My Emerald Green Dress

Alister Ramírez Márquez

TRANSLATED BY:
ALICIA BRALOVE

PROLOGUE BY:
GRACE CAVALIERI

Praise for *My Emerald Green Dress*

"A brilliant novel."

-STEPHEN VIZINCZEY, author of *Truth and Lies in Literature* (England)

"A wondrous and soulful novel."

-SABINE PASCARELLI, Italian poet (Italy)

"It is an intense, magical, and deeply human story."

-CARMEN CASANOVAS, Spanish literary agent (Spain)

"It is a testimony of a Latin American woman, which is at the same time the voice of many unknown women in the world."

-ESPERANZA JARAMILLO, Colombian poet (Colombia)

"The readers feel that they are part of the story, and often times invisible protagonists of *My Emerald Green Dress*."

-EMILIO GONZÁLEZ. Film and Television producer and critic, Canal Sur, Andalucía (Spain)

"An outstanding novel. After reading it, I gave to my wife and she could not stop reading it."

-ÁLVARO MUTIS, Colombian writer (México)

"It is like entering the world of One Thousand and One Nights. It is not only one book, but many books; it is not only one story but *My Emerald Green Dress* tells many stories."

-HILARIO RODRÍGUEZ, Film critic, ABC (Spain)

"The characters and the plot are very well developed. One can feel and touch them. Without dramas Alister

Ramírez Márquez shows us Colombian reality during the 20th century."
　　-PLINIO APULEYO MENDOZA, Colombian writer (Portugal)

"It is a deeply human intense story. Clara is one of those characters who is just unforgettable."
　　-REINALDO MARCHANT, Chilean writer (Chile)

"His prose is sensitive poetry. It is a precious emerald green jewel."
　　-JAIME QUEZADA, Chilean Poet (Chile)

"*My Emerald Green Dress* is an astounding novel. The reader must find irresistible not only the charming prose but also the culinary recipes, the local customs, flavors, smells, and homemade medicines."
　　-LUIS EDUARDO GALLEGO, Colombian historian (Colombia)

"The novel reflects on a topic that was forgotten in Latin American literature: different aspects of the history of internal migration, hundreds of people forced to move from the countryside to towns."
　　-ENRIQUE SERRANO, Colombian writer (Colombia)

"Alister Ramírez Márquez takes us to the violent history of Colombia. From Clara's point of view we can enter this chaotic word without tears or reproaches."
　　-MIRIAM COTES BENÍTEZ, *Boletín Cultural y Bibliográfico*. Biblioteca Luis Ángel Arango, Bogotá (Colombia)

"Alister Ramírez Márquez is capable of irony for he writes us a convention vast with violence at the heart of its characters that is at the same time brilliantly colored."
　　-GRACE CAVALIERI, poet, critic, playwright (U.S.A.)

"Clara is neither a hero nor a victim. She is a woman like many others."

-HERBERT BRAUN, historian (U.S.A.)

"A splendid and extraordinary novel."

-IDA RUBIN, curator and art critic (U.S.A.)

Alister Ramírez Márquez is an American citizen who was born in Colombia. He has a Ph.D in Hispanic Literature from The Graduate Center of The City University of New York. Previously published works are: Reportaje a once escritores norteamericanos (Planeta Editorial, 1996), ¿Quién se robó los colores? (Wayside, Massachusetts 1999, Second Edition Wayside 2009), Mi vestido verde esmeralda (Ala de Mosca, 2003, Stockcero 2006), winner of the 2005 Best International Literary Prize by the Art Critics Circle of Chile, Andrés Bello: crítico (Ala de Mosca, 2005), and his most recent novel is: Los sueños de los hombres se los fuman las mujeres (Planeta Editorial, 2009). Ramírez Márquez is a professor of Spanish and Hispanic American literature at The City University of New York, Borough of Manhattan Community College. He is a contributor for one of the major newspapers in Latin America, El Tiempo of Colombia.

My Emerald Green Dress

by
ALISTER RAMÍREZ MÁRQUEZ

Translation from Spanish by
ALICIA BRALOVE

FOREST WOODS MEDIA

Original title: Mi vestido verde esmeralda

First Edition in Spanish: 2003
First Annotated Edition in Spanish: 2006
First Edition in English: 2010
First Edition in Italian: 2010

ISBN: 0938572512
ISBN-13: 9780938572510

For Alicia, Richard, Alistair,
Darwin and all women who have
fighter spirit

TABLE OF CONTENTS

My Emerald Green Dress

PROLOGUE

This novel written in Spanish and translated into Italian comes to us now in English. Nietzche reminds us that language creates the value of its culture. Translation defies the stable meaning of each word, because no word is ever stable to begin with. There is no absolute meaning for a word in any language for all time. So the translation of this book is a miraculous combination of the transference of thought and nuance several times over. In spite of the temporality of language from one state of being to another, the context can remain clear. So it is with this adventure story that begins in 1900 and follows the life of a woman through an odyssey of struggle, hardship, adventure and transformation.

In film we talk about the "character driven" story, and indeed this describes the book, *My Emerald Green Dress*. If we were to consolidate the story line, it can be said that Ana María Ramona Clarisa (Clara) born at the dawn if the 20th century in Colombia (Angelópolis) entered a world that was impoverished, materially and intellectually. One of six children, who were separated when the mother died, Clara and her sister were in the care of her aunt. The early years are marked by meager schooling and pitiful conditions. Terrible also was her first love experience with Domingo, a relationship of abuse to the point of torture. It is no wonder she marries an older man, Jesús Márquez, a mule driver, and follows him from the more civilized coastal areas of Colombia through the mountains and wilderness of the interior country. Her life then is one of a hard felicity raising the children of Jesús, and having her own. The novel carries us forward to each child's adulthood, the birth of her grandchildren, on to old age and illness. The 2008 Nobel Prize winner for Literature, Le Clézio, once remarked -- of a hard-bitten and cruel existence -- "It is all so precious. So precious." And so it is in this, a novel of pictorial meanings, shared sympathy with the land, plant life, and wild creatures, made up of sufferings that are "precious" because of our understandings of them.

I come to this book as a lover of Italo Calvino so I feel at home. The state of this novel's art form is unadorned and bears a beautiful austerity. It cares not for the reader's fears and desires, because the conditions are ruthless and the world we are shown almost savage. It is a cauldron of human ambition, greed, and stupidity in some ways transformed by tenacity and courage, and the bold theory that a woman can become the protagonist in a pioneer story.

It's contrary to logic to enjoy a novel of someone's misery (yet we seem to do so with Dickens,) and we cannot debate that the mind longs for comfort along the way. Yet this writer, Alister Ramírez Márquez, is capable of irony, for he writes us a convention vast with violence at the heart of its characters that is at the same time brilliantly colored. Clara does not despair. She is a feminist before the term was coined. She conquers the land, makes her way in the material world, and we find the scope of her world is never larger than her capacities to endure, and more than that, to win over existing conditions.

How does any rebirth or translation of language suit senseless and crass behavior? This is a fairy tale but it is a fairy tale of a primitive society. Despair is understood. Despair is the place where all lost things go. But those prepared for disappointment by being born into it, have the gift of what can be understood by it. And with that, they have the prescription for what can be obtained. The language in the novel suits the story; sensations are broad brush connections because refinement does not exist. The language reflects the values of its people. This is a reality created for us, populated with people, cruel, rough, longing for beauty, but the voice in the writing is strong - and makes them strong. It depicts the human condition through characters that cross the Colombian mountains, that venture into Argentina, and Mexico. Although the story peaks at the time of the Peróns in Argentina, I believe it goes on today. This book, as if it is memory, lives in the Colombian forests, and in a world where folklore is the bible, superstition is religion, and fantasy, the layers between.

If there is a philosophical reality to all writing, it is that time is a thin line moving between life and death, and that sorrow is its process. In depicting this, however, can we find delight? Yes. Is there lyricism to be found when entering this hard land? Absolutely.

I am pleased to enter the magic reality of Alister Ramírez Márquez because these are people I would never know. I feel sure they exist today in Latin America, in Appalachia America, in all rural parts of Europe. This is a look at people beginning with lives whose endings are not safe. The way is then always hazardous. The description of such lives is where we enter the land of "carrying through" "carrying through life" in some way, in any way possible. We savor the culture that is not our own. That is where, in this book, I entered the forest of the unknown. I hope someday, some scholar will be able to hold the volumes of *My Green Emerald Dress*, Spanish, Italian, English, page by page and side by side, to view the temporality of language from one tongue to another, and to see with amazement that the consequence of "story" is held intact. This, then, is the mark of a true writer.

GRACE CAVALIERI *is a poet, critic, playwright. She produces and hosts "The Poet and the Poem from the Library of Congress" for public radio.*

PART I

Chapter I

CLARA

When I brought my cousin Venicia and her husband to these lands, she told me that I was born in 1900, and I believed her.

The priest in Angelópolis baptized me with the names Ana María Ramona Clarisa, but my aunt always called me Clara. She was the one who raised my sister Antonia and me because our mother died when she gave birth to me. My father parceled out my five other sisters to the rest of the relatives, and I never heard from any of them except when my oldest sister died.

My father was a miner whom I saw only a few times in my life because after my mother passed away, he wanted nothing more to do with us. He used to tell my aunt that as soon as he found gold in Llanos de la Clara, he would come back for us. But after her brother left she would tell us, getting angrier each time that he was good for nothing.

My sister and I attended the only school in Llanos de la Clara. There were ten students, a teacher, and three benches. It had a dirt floor, and the teacher, Señorita Chantal, made us sweep every inch of it with a grass broom. She claimed she was French, but she came from Amagá. She had bulging eyes like my aunt's cow, and practically never smiled, even when the thatched roof fell in on her and we all burst our sides laughing.

She had long, dirty fingernails and couldn't hide how much children disgusted her.

I learned to read but not to write. I didn't discover how much fun it was to write until I was a grown woman. Even though I had no idea what Señorita was saying, I would chime in on the choruses of *Abisorba, Abisorparba*...which was an exercise for learning the ABCs. She also used to speak of the wisdom of Don José Manuel Marroquín and the bravery of General Rafael Uribe Uribe. After repeating "one piece of coal plus one piece of coal" over and over again in school so many times, I grasped the power of addition, and was able to keep track at home of exactly how many cornmeal cakes I made and how many eggs the hens laid in a month. There weren't a lot of eggs, so my aunt saved them to sell in the market. Although she said the brown ones were best, of course I didn't understand what she meant by that until sometime later when I made my first friend.

My sister Antonia and I shared a bed and my aunt slept on the floor because of back pain. One dawn, just a few seconds before waking up, it seemed to me that I was drowning in an icy puddle and that a little girl who looked a lot like me was trying to drag me out of the water. When I woke up, Antonia had pulled the whole tattered blanket over herself. Then, all of a sudden, somebody was touching my feet and I could tell their hands were warm because of the contrast with my cold skin. At first I thought it was my aunt, but I was able see her there on the floor. I went back to sleep because I figured it must have been the little dog we had that licked our faces and feet in the morning. When my aunt woke us up, she told me that Anita had died. I had no idea who Anita was, but by the way my aunt described her, it seemed to me that she looked very much like the girl in my dream. Anita was my oldest sister, and we found out from my father that she had been running high fevers from malaria for a long time.

My aunt got us up at four o'clock every morning to grind corn and make cornmeal cakes. I hated that big stone mortar because I could barely lift the heavy wooden pestle. Antonia would help me, and finally I was able to manage very well. By six o'clock we'd had breakfast and were ready for the one-hour hike to school. We had no shoes, so the chiggers got into our feet. As for the ticks that clamped on to our legs and sucked the blood, we were able to pick them off by pouring hot water over them.

My only dress was a simple piece of thin cotton material that I had to wash every day. One time, I couldn't go to school because it rained without a letup, and my dress didn't dry. Antonia managed to get out a skirt out of my aunt's trunk without her knowing, and tied the skirt around me with a piece of henequen rope. I hung around Don José María Giraldo's stables all that day because I didn't want the other children laughing at me. All in all, we were a disturbance for Señorita Chantal, like warts on her nose, but she ended up getting used to her flock of dwarves in adult-size hand-me-downs.

Don José María Giraldo owned a lot of cattle in Llanos de la Clara and sold brown sugar to the people in La Estrella, Heliconia, Titiribí, Amagá, and Angelópolis, where we were from. His daughter Nera went to our school. She was four years older than me, almost the same age as my sister Antonia. Nera received special treatment from Señorita Chantal. It didn't matter that she was the tallest; she got seated on the front bench. Nera didn't talk to any of us, and if the teacher asked her a question, she would only stammer. Señorita Chantal would just smile whenever she spoke to her, and acted like she was Nera's maid. Don José María had hired her as his daughter's private teacher but, in view of Nera's mental problems, the priest convinced him to send her to our little school. Her father agreed that it would be better for her to be together with other children in a schoolroom even though they were from miners' families. The priest's idea was that she should be with

3

youngsters her own age. Don José María, who founded the chapel in Angelópolis, was asked to set up a little school in one of his brown sugar storehouses. He agreed on one condition: that Nera would not talk to the other children.

Señorita Chantal was there for just that purpose, and it was something she could put her heart into. One day, I couldn't stand having that head of gorgeous ringlets in my face any longer. They were blocking my view of the blackboard which prevented me from showing off how smart I was. So I let her know she didn't own the school. Opening her mouth for the first time as if to talk, Nera squawked like a gosling trying out its first gabbles, and then she burst out crying. The tears welled up from so deep inside her and with such force that her lacy dress was soaked from top to bottom. Señorita Chantal had to send for Don José María, and the child was taken home on a stretcher.

I couldn't go back to my aunt's house with Antonia that night. The teacher had locked me in the brown sugar storeroom but, before leaving, she had scattered kernels of corn all over the floor and made me crawl around on my knees until I'd said the Lord's Prayer fifty times. There in the dark storeroom, I found the teacher's desk with a cheese cornmeal cake on it sent by Don José María for his daughter, and I ate it. I had peed from fright, but didn't care so long as I could get out of there. After piling up the benches one on top of another, I was able to poke my head out through the opening that remained from when the roof fell in on Señorita. That night, I felt my way along the paths which I knew by heart, and was able to get to my aunt's house around daybreak.

My aunt decided to stop sending me to school because she considered it a waste of my time and besides she needed help with the housework. My sister told me that Nera never went back to the school, and that Señorita Chantal would get mad all the time and scream at the eight pupils that she hadn't come to this graveyard to put up with brats and she was not a nursemaid for a crazy girl who believed in the devil. And who did that snotty kid think she was- an angel from Notre Dame? Neither my sister nor I knew what Notre Dame was, but I figured it must be the place where the Señorita came from.

The next time I saw Nera, she was sixteen years old. I was minding my aunt's cow, as it grazed on Don José María's pastures. My aunt paid him a hundred cornmeal cakes, made every day by us, of course, in exchange for the goat's rue and pigweed that was churned up in the cow's four stomachs. Nera, sitting on a hill, had on a white dress and shoes her father had bought for her in Madrid. I knew because she told me so. It was the first time in my life I'd ever seen such shoes. She was more beautiful and silent than ever, but didn't ignore me, and called me Clarita. At first I thought it was the cow talking, and felt as though the roots of the grass were going to get tangled in my toenails and pull me under and bury me because I always had the idea Nera was mute. My name sounded so strange to me because nobody ever said it with "*ita*" tacked on. And even more surprising, she laughed at how pale I had turned and told me that she was no ghost but was Don José María's daughter. She knew who I was, and thanked me for her having been taken out of the school. Later on, she told me that she, too, hated Señorita Chantal, that her name was really Encarnación, that she had gone to Paris as her father's assistant where she learned a couple of French words, and when she got back to Amagá told everybody that she was French.

The teacher's mother was an old charcoal seller nicknamed *La Chinca* because she was so little and peddled charcoal door to door. My aunt knew *La Chinca* and had heard her telling Señorita Chantal—it felt like listening to the dead woman herself talking— that she knew what sickness it was that had killed her mother. According to my aunt, Doña Chinca had died of breaditis. I asked her what that word meant, and my aunt answered that it meant a disease you can get from bread. Señorita's mother ate nothing but unleavened bread and that's what killed her, eating so much bread. I believed everything my aunt told me, and wouldn't touch a crumb of it for the rest of my life, even though there's nothing like a well toasted cornmeal cake. We were poor as church mice. After her mother passed away, Don José María took Chantal in, not out of charity, but because he needed a servant in the house.

Nera talked nonstop, the cow ate everything within reach, and I couldn't tear my eyes away from those shoes of hers. When the afternoon was over, Nera took them off and gave them to me. After that, we would meet every day at the same time. I would just look at her as she told stories like about the time Don José María, the priest, and the notary had to get her down from the top of a caracolí tree.

"You know, Clarita, my daddy didn't want it known, but the truth is that I wanted to go off with a demon and my daddy kneeled down before him and begged him not to take me away. The demon agreed, and left me snagged on the treetop. But I know he'll be back, sooner or later."

Another time, Nera uncovered her chest to show me the proof that she had been kidnapped on that caracolí tree. There were purple lines on it that looked like an imprint from a hand with six fingers. Nera had eggs tucked away in her pockets and asked me to smear the whites on her breasts to ease the pain. I swallowed the yolks, and my aunt's cow ate the shells.

I made friends with Don José María's daughter on account of the brown sugar cubes she pulled out like magic from under her lace dress and, of course, there were the eggs. In any case, my main reason for listening to the caracolí story over and over again was so I could look at her collection of photographs. Each day, she would bring a different one to show me that she kept in a book that had the word *Faust* for a title. I knew that the book couldn't be in Spanish because; of the few words I had learned in school, none matched up with the ones on those mysterious pages. Then I found out that she was reading in German because years later, a foreign neighbor accused of owning evil books showed me another of those same books written in that same unreadable language.

The first picture Nera showed me was of a bishop, taken in Medellín. I'd never been in that city and figured that everybody there used a black cape and wore rings as costly as the one on the bishop's right hand. He was her uncle on her father's side and wanted Nera to enter a convent in Spain. Another photograph was of a group of men watching the dissection of a cadaver. According to Nera, her grandfather on her mother's side had been a doctor in Amsterdam. But the picture that surprised me the most was of her mother sitting in gardens somewhere. I had never seen her mother and suspected for a while that she might have been Señorita Chantal, but I was glad to find out I was wrong. Nera could never have been an outgrowth of that scarecrow. Actually, Nera had inherited her mother's beauty and elegance. She told me that her mother was from Granada, and that the photographs were taken at the Generalife gardens there. I had never seen flowers, orange trees, grapes or a fountain before. She would describe the colors to me, but I didn't know whether she was telling me the truth or not because the pictures were black and white. The only flowers I knew were wild flowers, yet the photograph she showed me was not of one of those, but of an orchid. I found out because Nera had pointed them out to me on tree trunks in a ravine, and I excused my aunt's ignorance who barely knew the difference between an armadillo and a turtle.

I remember the orchid very well because it was growing in the middle of my aunt's pigsty. That poor sow of ours was so skinny that in an uncontrollable act of desperation, she bit it off leaving no evidence of the crime on her snout. It made me angry, but also jealous, because at the same time that I felt sorry for the sow, I understood her. For her, the orchid represented the equivalent of what cracklings were to me, and I got to eat them once a year.

Nera's mother did not want to return to the mountains and her father ended up accepting the loss of his wife. Don José María raised Nera and Señorita Chantal was her nurse and private teacher.

One of Nera's favorite pastimes was to show me her mother's photograph in the gardens and invent stories, as though she were a famous person. In one of the stories, the woman was the image of a favorite slave in Sultan Yasuf's harem, and one day the sultan found out that this slave had a lover in the court. The couple met secretly in the Generalife gardens. Nobody knew who the lover was. The sultan summoned his thirty-six warriors, and cut their heads off. Another was that Yasuf lived in a red castle. He only had carpets in his room, and the name written on the wall of the one who had helped him win the war. One of the slaves in the harem approached her master, knelt before him, and said: "I am a Christian; they kidnapped me and sold me in Africa." The sultan answered. "You are now in the land of Allah." That night the Christian slave threw herself from the watchtower.

Nera taught me the meaning of the Arabic words *aljibe, alcazaba, arrayán, albaicín alcázar* or *alhambra*. The closest familiar word to me in my language was *alambre*, wire, because Don José María had brought some of the barbed kind from Medellín to fence off his land.

Sometimes she listened to me, and enjoyed my story about a man who told fortunes with a parakeet every day in the market. One Sunday, it so happened that after mass my aunt took me and my sister to the square. I slipped away while my aunt was measuring out some corn in Don José María's barn. On the only through street in town, a man was shouting "My name is Domingo...I'm the Sunday, fortune-teller!"

I walked over and, being so little, was able to push my way through the crowd to the front. Domingo had a tripod with a little cage on it out of which a parakeet would waddle holding a paper in its beak. Nera had given me a few coins, and I decided to invest them in my fortune. The parakeet was so old it could hardly walk any longer, but it did manage to get through its performance with Domingo having to practically nudge it out of the cage.

"Ladies and Gentlemen: Darío, the parakeet, is concentrating... Darío, Darío..."

Domingo was looking at me uneasily, obviously with no intention of returning my money if I were to ask for it back. Finally, the little bird appeared with the tiny paper and Domingo snatched it from his beak before Dario could change his mind.

"Ladies and gentlemen, this girl will be going off to other lands, she will meet a prince, and live in a palace like Queen María Luisa's." The audience laughed and somebody called out that there weren't any princes or palaces where she was.

The hooting of the crowd attracted my aunt's attention, and when she walked over to see what was going on, she spotted me. She had hands like grappling hooks; she grabbed the man by the neck and warned him that if he was thinking of robbing me he would have her to reckon with. My punishment for having run off was to skin all the kernels of corn she had bought in the market. She also muttered something to the effect that if I expected to be rich, I would have to marry a merchant like Don José María.

The last time I saw Nera was when I said goodbye to her, because I was eloping with Domingo. She gave me the photograph of her mother in the Generalife gardens, as well as a bag full of eggs, brown sugar, cornmeal cakes, and fried cheese. I told her I would be going with him to Medellín, then to Puerto Berrío, and after that on the boat to Barranquilla. Domingo had told me he had relatives in Madrid who, sooner or later, would be taking us in. We would get married in Santa Ana Church there and he would show me the gardens of Generalife.

But we didn't even get as far as Marinilla because he dumped me, with nothing to my name but Darío, the parakeet, nearly dying of bronchitis. I was thirteen years old at the time and no longer a virgin.

Chapter II

DOMINGO

The night I said goodbye to Antonia my aunt and her sow were both sound asleep on the floor. The difference between the sow's sleep and my aunt's was that the animal's was induced by depression and my aunt's simply by fatigue. The pig wasn't worth anything even at the slaughterhouse, but my aunt thought that by selling her she might get some money for us to buy shoes. Antonia didn't want to leave with me because she had grown very fond of the old woman, and we were all she had in the world.

I liked Domingo from the first moment I saw him. I don't know whether it was on account of his not being from around here, or because of a resemblance to my father, at least what I remembered of him. He was more than three times my age, stood taller than the other miners I had seen, had a neatly trimmed black mustache, and did not wear a poncho the same way as everybody else did. He smoked cigarettes, and even while reading out the little fortune papers had one dangling from his lips. From the way my aunt saw me eye him on the street, she knew I liked him. There wasn't a thing she could do to shut that attraction down. Even though she nearly strangled him, the fellow was so charming that he won my aunt over by having the little parrot, Dario, let her know her that she had been chosen by good fortune and that money for a business would soon be coming her way. And so, when Don José María agreed to buy her pig, my aunt was convinced that her luck was at last changing.

Like my aunt, I believed Domingo, and we would meet on the sly every weekend after mass. Antonia came with me while my aunt sold eggs in the square. One afternoon, he proposed that I go off with him, and I didn't think twice. The idea of being kidnapped fascinated me. So I made a pact with Antonia to tell my aunt that Domingo had kidnapped me, and taken me to Spain. If a demon had picked out Nera to carry off to his world, why couldn't I be the victim of a handsome and charming man like him?

The first night we ran away, Domingo and I walked over the back paths of Don José María's property. I knew those trails perfectly, and the main thing was to get as far away as possible so as not to give my aunt time to follow us. After walking for two days, we came to an inn near La Estrella. Doña Nicasia fixed us a nest on the floor with brown sugar sacks, and we slept there for several hours. I had never slept with anybody before other than my sister, certainly not a man. When I woke up, I examined my breasts to see if there were purplish lines on them like Nerita's, but there were no marks of any kind on my body. Doña Nicasia told me that Domingo had gone to Fredonia, and would be back in two days. He did return, and I hardly recognized him; Dario wasn't with him, his mustache was all matted like the sow's hair, and his voice had no ring at all to it like when he shouted: "I'm Domingo, the Sunday fortune-teller." He punched me in the mouth so hard that it split my lips and left my face swollen for days, and then he tore off me the only little rag dress that I owned.

He shaved every morning, combed his mustache, brushed his frock coat, and made me polish his boots. He didn't speak to me, and told Doña Nicasia that he was going to pay her for "the girl's food" at the end of the month. He would come back drunk at night, and give me a beating before raping me. Even though the old woman pushed dishes of food to me under the door, I couldn't eat. Sometimes I would swallow a bit of fried banana which reminded me of my aunt's sow and the way the poor thing was kept locked up, and how she could hardly raise herself on her hind legs and munch a bit of fried banana with what was left of her teeth. One day, the landlady, tired of waiting for Domingo who hadn't been back for three weeks, opened the door to my room that was tied up outside with a rope, and said, "Get up, child. Stop crying. May evil spirits come and swallow that Domingo alive!"

I looked up and saw that Doña Nicasia was holding Darío. She handed him to me, and left the door open. Dario couldn't stop coughing, but Doña Nicasia brought us both around with brown sugar water and lemon that she prepared each day.

"My dear, you're a very strong girl, and a few days on pigeon broth will chipper you up."

Domingo didn't come back, and not for a second did I miss him. Since I had no clothes, Doña Nicasia gave me an army jacket that had belonged to her deceased husband. My aunt had taught me sewing, and so I took apart that relic of the Thousand Day War and made myself a dress out of it. The cloth was worn thin, and had blood stains that I was able to hide in the hem. The buttons were rotted out, but I was able to replace them with ivory-palm seeds that I had gathered. Doña Nicasia needed help at the inn with the meals for the guests, upkeep of the stable and laundry. I was like a daughter to her, and even though I missed Nera, the cow, Antonia, my aunt, and the pig, I felt comfortable in my new home. I couldn't go back anyway because the distances were huge, and the roads were wiped out by the washouts.

I got used to the routine of the inn, and I also earned tips from the mule drivers. I decorated kerchiefs for them with avocado dye which they took home as a fine present for their wives. I would save the avocado seeds and when they gave me a piece of material, I would spread it over the pit, and by pricking it through the cloth with a needle, I'd make the maroon dye come out. Since I was the only one who knew the alphabet and some other words, they paid me good money for their ignorance. Doña Nicasia had an avocado tree in the patio. It was no taller than the caracolí that the demon dropped Nera on, which she once showed me and assured me was the same blessed tree. The avocados picked from that tree weighed over three pounds each, were just like butter inside, and oozed a milky-white juice when I opened them. I got so fond of avocados that I ate them for breakfast, sliced them into the beans, into the soup, and even washed my hair with avocado soap that I made myself. Domingo had pulled out bunches of my hair, but rubbing avocado on the bare spots made new roots come up. Doña Nicasia had me pick the avocados with a hoe before they fell from the branches because they were so big that they looked like chamber pots hanging by the handle. I cut them in half, removed the hearts and used the seed before it dried out because if you wait too long, the dye doesn't stain.

Mule drivers came from Medellín. Some had pockets and sacks filled with combs, lace, and cigarettes, others were transporting loads of brown sugar to unfamiliar lands. It was a world of men shifting from place to place like shadows. Those who arrived at the inn slept like men, got drunk like men, played cards and dice like men, told stories like men, and went on their way like men. I always wondered what their conversations were about on the roads during those endless trips. Sometimes I thought it was the mules talking, and the men carrying the loads on their shoulders. Long afterwards, I became aware of the fascination of the silence on rainy days and the echo of the birds in new places. It was like a pilgrimage of silence. The only intervals were made up of the sound of voices and the men's laughter at night around the stove of Doña Nicasia's inn. They returned from the new lands as though bewitched, with that same look as my father's on their faces, but many pilgrims stayed on for good.

One of the mule drivers who had given me an order to put his wife's initials on some bed sheets did not return that year. However, he had paid in advance, so I sent them on to him with one of his comrades. Twenty months later, he was back at the inn with a load of potatoes. He was on his way to Medellín to buy ammunition, and would be returning to the new lands with ten sacks of brown sugar. He told me that his wife had died, and that was why he hadn't returned. His name was Jesús, he had eyes like a cat, skin tanned by the sun, was thirty years older than me and....I liked the kerchiefs he always brought me from Medellín. One night I noticed him whispering to Doña Nicasia and while I was serving him beans, he asked me, shyly, like a small boy, if I would go with him. Doña Nicasia had told me that it was true about him being a widower and about his six children who were practically my age. But the most important thing was that Don Jesús owned a lot of property in the new lands. What Doña Nicasia did not tell me, however, was that he had done ten years in prison for killing the mayor of a village, and that it took him six months on mule back to get back to his lands.

I told Jesús that I would think it over, and he returned the following year for the answer. I nodded my head yes and set only one condition: that he promise to marry me in any church whatsoever. He kept his promise, but not until after our first child was born, and then because I nearly died during the delivery. The priest and notary were on hand that night, one to give me last rites, and the other to draw up a will in which I appeared as Don Jesús Márquez's lawfully wedded wife, in which case my son would have the right of inheritance. But the priest didn't use the extreme unction oils and married us instead.

Don Jesús needed a wife to help bring up his children, and who would be waiting for him in bed. I was not really the most cut out for this, but convinced myself that it was best for me. Besides, the old fellow was a charming man; he was like my father or, at least my memory of daddy Lázaro. Jesús never held my not being a virgin against me, and at his age, it no longer mattered to him. After living with Jesús, I never had nightmares again of racing naked on cliffs that bordered on rivers of shit. Domingo was wiped completely out of my mind.

Doña Nicasia sent us off with her blessing, and I gave her Darío, the parakeet. Our procession consisted of twenty mules loaded with food and a shotgun that Jesús slung over my back as a present to celebrate our union. Over the course of the long journey he taught me to shoot and for a beginner, my aim was not at all bad.

Chapter III

THE TREK

The rain didn't let up for a single day in the first month. I knew it was April because Jesús kept repeating that this was the Easter Week rain. Except for stops to stretch our legs and have a bite to eat, the trek continued each day until dark. My mount, a mare, was quite broad in the beam and I, not being an experienced rider, had to keep my seat by constant pressure on her flanks. After two weeks or so, I got the hang of it, and she would neigh in appreciation. Fortunately for her I didn't weigh much, and my luggage consisted of nothing but a sack for my belongings: a dress Jesús had bought me, and the shoes Nera gave me.

In the evening, Jesús sought out a kapok tree to protect us from the rain. I slept clinging to him like a tick as we lay in the midst of our animals for warmth. I couldn't see his face, but did smell his tobacco breath. Jesús would tell me stories of hunting in the mountains like the time when, although his mules were swept away by the river, he had miraculously escaped with his life and, fortunately, his shotgun, so he could shoot game and survive. There were ocelots in those mountains that camouflaged themselves among the brambles but Jesús, agile like a cat himself, could spot the glint in the eyes of his feline relatives. He told about how one time while kneeling at a stream to drink, he sensed an animal very close by cautiously stalking its prey, which was him. With no time to think, taking lightning-fast aim, he sent a shot dead into the wildcat's face. This gave him food enough till he met up with some treasure hunters. Jesús didn't have to convince me of his bravery; I loved his stories.

We were up before dawn each day. I would make coffee for everyone over a hasty little fire. At the outset we traveled alone, but on the fourth week out or so, we were joined by another group of mule drivers on their way to the new lands, and the caravan grew. I had no idea how long we were climbing those muddy mountain trails, but I was almost immediately petrified when I turned around and looked down. Jesús had told me to always look straight ahead and not to worry. Nevertheless, I felt like my eyes had switched over to the back of my head. It was as though the gap between the world I had left behind and this traveling world was widened more and more by the voids formed by the abysses which, thank God, I wouldn't see again. With my mule's every stride, the orange-tinted earth was transformed. Every stone, every age-old fern, every cubic millimeter of water that seeped through those mountain walls changed its place as we pressed on, leaving my life behind like an empty eggshell.

Jesús had learned to read my panic signals, but this time he did not want to stop the caravan until we reached the mountain top, so we spent the night there and he tried to take advantage of the opportunity to go hunting with the other men. How silly of them to think I would stay behind with the mules! I went with the men and let the mules rest since they were tired from a long day's work.

At night, we could hear the tapirs bellowing, the fluttering of huge moths with eyes like owls, and bats screeching joyously as they landed on stalks of little bananas. Jesús was terrified of those nocturnal birds. He called them vampires because they sucked the animals' blood by biting, especially at the legs of the mules. What worried him the most about those creatures of the night was that he had no way of saving their human victims. A mule driver of his had died on one of those treks because he had not been given first aid in time and the poor fellow bled to death.

Jesús told me that he himself had been bitten one time by a vampire on the big toe of his right foot. However, he had washed the wound with boiling water, and then cut out the flesh with his pocket knife. He said that the main thing was to keep the bat saliva from entering at the site of the bite, which prevented the blood from coagulating and the patient from bleeding to death. Another way of stopping the hemorrhage was to put ashes or coffee grounds on the wound. At the same time, Jesús had an irresistible craving for bat meat. When he hunted them, he would cut their heads off and cook them in a stew. The vampire bats were white and fat and if not for their snout and bulging eyes, one could mistake the meat for guinea hen. I never tasted them myself, but Jesús said that if it weren't for their bloody traits, he would have set up a hatchery because they were cheaper than chickens or turkeys and ate bananas. When he trapped them alive he would bring them to me, and right in front of me have one man hold a bat up by the end of one wing and another man by the end of the other wing while he lit a cigarette and offered it to the creature. It was amazing to watch the way it not only offered no resistance but puffed on the cigarette with apparent enjoyment. Jesús and the other men seemed given to such almost childish diversions and expected me to laugh along with them in their fun, but I found it repulsive like watching mules die in a pool of their own blood.

As for the ants, darkness and light are all the same to them, and armies of them mobilized with organizational tactics that enabled them to destroy the bark off even a guava tree. There are many varieties of ants: black, brown, blonde, reddish, tiny and some so big they could practically juggle a ball of horse manure. Ants would get into my sack and trousers, into the leaves the meat was wrapped in, into the shotgun barrels, and the eyelashes of the mules. I couldn't avoid getting the notion that I was seeing them everywhere and, when I had nothing better to do, I would follow the trails they made. Each of the millions of ants that passed before my eyes carried a bit of a leaf or a cricket wing. If the load was very heavy, the weight was borne by several of them, the same way the strongest miners of Angelópolis carry the Virgin on their backs up the slope to the altar of the church during the Easter processions. Each insect transported a piece of the load; for example, they would stuff a whole guava into their tunnels, and it was as though they had inserted the soul of the tree in the hollows they made in the mud. Jesús considered ants pests; in the rainy season even more so. Some were as big as bees and with a sting that was mortal. I had learned to tell them apart and, most important, to avoid them.

Jesús had taken on some hunting dogs at Doña Nicasia's inn. They were hounds with long ears and short coats. I had never seen these hunters in action, but when it came to their work, they became the center of attention and directed our efforts. Their snouts were like their eyes and ours as well. They would find nests everywhere, which they tore apart looking for chicks or eggs. It was like training for a race. Jesús had told me not to be fooled by eyes shining in the night. They did not always belong to ocelots, but often to mice, weasels, rabbits or guinea pigs. The pupils of felines, however, shine in a special way, and the animal has to be attacked before it springs. I was the first to observe this because it had that same look as Jesús when he got nervous. The animal went for one of the dogs' throat and killed it in a matter of seconds. It was all so fast that I don't know when or why I shot at a shadow that moved across my vision. The ocelot, actually a female, lay dead with its fangs buried in the hound's throat. Jesús was terrified, and I could see his eyes shining in the darkness. He was as pale as a ghost. The other men took over handling the animal that weighed over a hundred fifty pounds and whose age Jesús guessed at three years. Her coat was very beautiful with large black spots on the head, back, and paws and these spots got smaller towards the belly and throat. Her claws reminded me of the marks on Nera's breasts because the lines on her chest were so thin and at the same time so deadly-looking that they did not appear to be the result merely of a little girl who scratched herself during an epileptic fit. It was as though that ocelot must have been sharpening its claws daily on the same walnut tree.

Of course the ocelot's stomach was empty, which explains why she attacked the dog with no regard for the consequences. The men told Jesús that it was unlucky to take a woman hunting especially one who had a red birthmark on her left cheek. Actually, I didn't remember what was on my face, and they made me conscious of both it and of my being a female. Jesús loved the birthmark inherited from my father, which he said was like a blackberry permanently at its ripest. I had never seen blackberries, and later on when he showed them to me in Salento, I thought he was making fun of me. The difference between my birthmark and my father's was that he had it on his right arm, and mine was like a drop of blood on a white handkerchief. I was very pale, and the birthmark stood out like a blackberry only when the weather turned very hot. I never saw my father's birthmark or the one on my grandmother's cheek, because I never knew her. My aunt said that it was the Lázaro mark, which was the last name of my mother's father's family.

The hunters and the rest of the mule drivers convinced Jesús that it was best that I, a woman with a red birthmark, stay behind with the mules when they went hunting. Though they stopped taking me along when they went hunting at night, I practiced shooting when nobody was around. During our trek the men didn't bring in anything but a few armadillos, guinea pigs, and monkeys. I could not get used to the sight of my husband with the head of a monkey in his two hands tearing ravenously with his teeth at the flesh on its skull. They skinned, cut up, and salted monkey meat. Salt was like magic for curing leftover meat which we wrapped up in smoked leaves. After a while, it was hard to tell the difference between a monkey leg and guinea pigs. I boiled beans and cooked the anthropomorphic game with citron. Citrons hung on the palm trees and I would climb up and pick them. Jesús would shake the trunk while I held onto the branches. The guava fruits and citrons would fall to the ground without bouncing. I would scream, and he would tell me I was going to scare the defenseless little sloths with my yelling.

I used monkey intestine to make sausages that were good for weeks and, in fact, the longer they were kept, the more delicious they tasted. Nothing went to waste. I would often see the mule drivers sucking their fingers, and I myself couldn't tell a monkey hand from a human one. Jesús would crunch even the finger bones. As for me, I enjoyed a soup I made of squash and turtle doves that I myself had hunted. Jesús taught me to how to be careful with prickly leaves and use the sprouts of the nettles instead for cooking.

The trek grew tiresome and unbearable, particularly when we went through valleys without trees. It was impossible to escape from the sun and starting from very early in the morning, the light would penetrate my closed eyelids and for a long time I had the feeling of having gotten no sleep because I was always exposed to endless glare. It was as if darkness no longer had a place in those stretches of unsettled lands. We quenched our thirst with a drink Jesús taught me to prepare. It consisted of drops of citric acid squeezed from lemons and dissolved in water. When it was too bitter, a chunk of brown sugar was added. Jesús also carried in his leather case quinine, opium, and a small flask of corn alcohol as a disinfectant for treating snakebites. One of the most dangerous snakes is called the shots. It was about a half a meter long and entered the bushes to attack its prey. I had already seen several mules topple to the ground after having stepped on one and been bitten. They are called shots because they are as deadly as a bullet and they have great aim when they strike. If their victims are not treated, poisoning is inevitable. I saw Jesús forced to shoot several animals because they were suffering the effect of the poison. Other muleteers had seen snakes with a head twice the size of Jesús' fist and one of my husband's trusted workers told me that once he saw one of them show its head in a corn patch, and he was too scared to approach. There were snakes in the rivers and when we crossed, we had to be on the watch because the bite of one of those could drive a horse crazy and might kill a man who was not trained to deal with such cases.

We almost always filled our gourds with rainwater in the valleys. We stored runoff water in makeshift cisterns. A hole was dug in the ground, filled with stones, and lined with banana leaves and the rainwater collected there. We used that water when we were not near a river. However, even though many muleteers are knowledgeable about determining water purity for both human and animal consumption, there is always a case of one of them coming down with yellow fever, diarrhea, and vomiting. Jesús had forbidden me to drink water from certain streams, particularly if the running water was black, and he also made me avoid stagnant water in the swamps, even if I was dying of thirst.

At night we protected ourselves from the mosquitoes with netting even if the heat didn't let us breathe because it was preferable to live with the sweat and avoid coming down with malaria. I had seen lots of crosses on our trek. Some had initials, others were blank. One of the first I came across was practically intact. I didn't notice it in the weeds at first, but it was fairly straight and in good condition despite the sun and the ants. I was struck by its size and the smoothness of the wood. It was not like the others along the road, and Jesús was sure that it was not a mule driver's grave but a treasure hunter's who never found gold but caught some disease instead. Jesús was also a professional treasure hunter. He considered many to be foolhardy and unaware of the dangers in the mountains. Members of several of his expeditions had died of fevers and dysentery. There had been barely enough time to bury them, but this grave seemed to belong to a leader of a group of treasure hunters. On reaching the nearest settlement, the survivors of the group would have notified the authorities and the priest, who conducted one mass in Latin for all souls since many deaths were not even reported or looked into.

There was another grave I can't forget, a child's. There was a ridge close to a river nearly a meter high where all the rocks were placed in such a way that they made what seemed like a solid block. Whoever made the burial wanted to make sure no storm would wipe out the memory of a life and, according to the data on the guava-wood cross, I could tell that it was of a newborn named Alcira. Three days after the birth, the mother also died because further on, I came across another grave bearing the name Alcira.

Jesús was not surprised to find that string of corpses along the way. Furthermore, the graves served as markers of the route, always leaving behind vestiges of the struggle against flood and drought. Some of those women had, like me, made the trek to the new lands with their husbands and children. Others got pregnant halfway along, but many never lived to reach their destination. Jesús was immune to disease but not me, and because the trip seemed never-ending, I often wondered if I was going to end up in a grave of stones like those. Jesús sensed my despair and always buoyed up my spirits with the reassurance in his eyes. Yet, how long could body and patience hold out? I was already anxious to be in one place and to stay there, no matter if it meant the top of a kapok tree to escape the shot snakes. I had an urgent need to get somewhere and dig myself into the ground like a cross, not to show that I was dead, but full of life. Jesús, however, insisted that we would be in Anserma in a matter of weeks. He laughed and said that a woman who didn't complain was a man.

Nevertheless, I did not resent the rain. Rather, my spirit found solace in the sound of raindrops on leaves and of the frogs that looked up into the sky as the water invaded their abodes. My complaint was prompted by the fact that Jesús apparently was not concerned about reaching a fixed place. When I would come upon the skeleton of a toad, I sensed inside me that those bones had belonged to one of nature's creatures. Who would identify my skeleton if nobody knew me anywhere? Of course, it was not easy to identify the remains of a toad because they were so big that anybody might take them for a puppy's. Jesús had taught me to recognize their various cries and to what family they belonged. There were poisonous toads that discharged whitish saliva. One night when I got up to pee, I stepped on one of those creatures and my right leg got smeared with a milky slime. Jesús washed it for me immediately with his corn liquor, but it soon swelled up. Years later I was to curse the time it occurred to me to go out in the dark because I disliked using a chamber pot. I think my varicose veins were caused by my stubbornness, not the toad slime. The brown and yellow speckled giant toad is harmless. Its flesh was very insipid and had to be heavily seasoned.

Chapter IV

THE LIGNUM VITAE TREE

Anserma only had a few houses and looked pretty much like Angelópolis. We stayed there for a few weeks to change mules, buy salt, tobacco, ammunition, and take on more hunting dogs. We'd been traveling for three months, and still had three to go. That is, if the storms would allow us to stay on route. I had no idea what the final destination was, and it didn't matter because life was taken up by continual hunting, crossings on hanging bridges, and having to abandon pack animals because the paths became passable only to people. Even the dogs were not able to withstand the washouts, and the trees were so huge that I could write the alphabet with my pocket knife around a trunk five hundred times so as not to forget the letters. One of the trees I admired most was the lignum vitae, which Jesús called the holy wood tree. It is smaller than a walnut tree, and its wood is just as resistant. Its bark was greenish, so if you ran your hands over the trunk, your palms would be stained green.

I liked the leaves which were similar to the madrone's, but the sight of a lignum vitae in full yellow bloom among fig trees, bamboo, and mammee trees was a break in the monotony of the world that unfolded before my eyes. Jesús was not interested in the yellow fruits, but in the bark, a chunk of which he tore off the trunk, cut into splinters, and set out in the sun to dry for a couple of days. He told me that the best remedy for lumps was to cook the splinters in boiling water, strain them through a piece of cloth, and drink the juice. The holy wood drink was effective only if taken on an empty stomach. Jesús told me that he had learned the recipe from the Indians because he personally had seen them cure serious diseases with lignum vitae drinks.

But an interesting thing I want to point out is that it was precisely in a lignum vitae tree all bursting in yellow, like the cloak of the Virgin that I saw for the first time an animal that looked like a bear hanging from a branch at the top of the tree. It was impossible to miss its bulky presence amid the blooms and it was also impossible to miss the animal's strange behavior in that it didn't take any notice of my yelling at it to wake it up. Its four limbs clutched onto the branch and its head hung down as if it were a tail. Jesús came over to me and told me not to bother it because it was sound asleep, and to prove this, he and the others shook the tree. The animal didn't even move in spite of all the noise. This animal was actually a sloth or as Jesús used to say ironically, a fast bear. It moved very, very slowly, which I can well understand because it could hardly stand up on its four legs. I saw this with my own eyes because Jesús climbed the lignum vitae and brought the sloth down on his back. Its arms and legs were thin, and the front paws had claws like a bird. It had a long neck and a little head with a face that looked like an owl's crossed with a monkey's. Its mouth was small and it fed on leaves, but only occasionally because it would eat nothing for weeks on end. The most incredible thing, though, was that it managed to stay alive. At night, it produced a song that scared me because it sounded like a wail coming from evil spirits. Actually, the voice was heard only in the darkness since during the day the creature was nothing but a dumb sack of black and white hair hanging from a tree. At various times on the journey we had sloths, but ended up forgetting about them because they were so silent.

Though the sloth had a home in the lignum vitae, I had no place to go where I could rest and sing with the same serenity of that animal. I realized that either on horseback or on foot, I was always in motion. It was as though the idea of permanence was just a dream, and that endless motion was an ongoing reality.

On some stretches we had to wait days for raging rivers to subside. May was the worst month, and I always prayed to Saint Bárbara to placate God's wrath. On several occasions the river swallowed mules because the loads of brown sugar dragged them under. At other times, we had to leave the animals on the opposite side of the ravine because we were waiting for replacements. I found myself hanging from one of those swings made of vines and preferred not to look down at the river bottom. Jesús was very clever at tying knots and could put together a chair in the blink of an eye. He always carried ropes in his knapsack that he used for making bridges, pulling down bamboo and tree trunks, dragging in trophies of the hunt, or tying up robbers.

Encounters in those mountains were rare, and anyone you happened to meet had to be a treasure hunter. But one afternoon, while we were waiting for a storm to blow over, a short man appeared who could have been taken for a boy were it not for his voice. He was very skinny, and kept closing his eyes each time before he spoke. He told my husband that he was a treasure hunter traveling with twenty others, but had gotten separated from his group and now couldn't find them. Jesús said nothing, but let him spend the night with our caravan. Some time afterward, he admitted to me that the reason he allowed him to stay was because he thought he was the Wandering Jew. That, Jesús explained, was a man who traveled the whole wide world and never stayed anywhere. Instinctively, I couldn't go along with the idea that anybody could suddenly appear out of nowhere in this no-man's land and furthermore that it would be at all possible for him to survive without a horse, a gun, and a chunk of brown sugar. I had developed a skin as thick as an ocelot's, and my body repelled mosquitoes. A frail-looking man like this one wouldn't be able to fight off the first fevers of malaria so common in this climate. Jesús would pick herbs of all kinds—unfamiliar to me—as he went along, stash them away in a sack, and when one in the group fell sick, he would get out his plants, crush them up, and have the patient swallow the greenish juice. I learned from him to appreciate the benefits of plantain for nerves, horsetail for my kidney pain, dandelion for digestion, orange and lemon blossoms as relaxants and of course, for the heart, garlic, even though it was hard to come by in these remote parts.

The man in a boy's body stayed with us for several nights. In the daytime he would disappear. Jesús was not concerned about him taking off, but what did bother him was that he wasn't able to confirm his suspicion about this wanderer's identity. When I asked where he was going off to, he answered that he was checking out colors of the ground to figure the chances of there being an Indian grave in the region. As a treasure hunter himself, Jesús knew very well from experience that it was impossible for there to be any Indian graves with buried treasure in that area. My husband never lost sight of him during the night, and he watched me, and I watched both of them. Even though Jesús had given me some of his clothes to wear so that I wouldn't attract any attention in that bunch of men, he noticed that several of them eyed me when I took off my straw hat and my long hair fell over my back. My masculine disguise worked during the day but at night, though it was possible to barely make out faces in the candlelight, I couldn't hide my feminine nature.

But what did he want from us? An animal, a shotgun or some chunks of pork? He ate leaves and acorns that he gathered on his daily excursions, and one day he accepted a sausage from me, I think just not to refuse, because I later saw one of the hounds chomping on it. One night before we went on our way, the river having now lowered, Jesús told the man that we were going to

Anserma, and that he could come with us if he liked, and from there he would have a better chance of locating his group. The man did not answer, but closed his eyes as usual as if to avoid contact with the world. Awakened by the cold at three in the morning, I realized that the fellow was nowhere to be found. Just as I suspected might happen, he had stolen my mare, Jesús's shotgun, and two boxes of cartridges. I woke Jesús, and he roused the others. Jesús always carried a knife strapped to his right leg, and I knew Jesús would chase him like an armadillo even if he had gone into the river. It was only a matter of hours: my husband was familiar with every inch of those leafy labyrinths and river banks.

"Nobody steals my shotgun and my wife's mare from me, and gets away with it" he raged.

The man didn't get very far before Jesús caught up with him trying to cross the river. He took him; hands behind his back, practically dragging him by a lasso attached to his horse, and handed him over to the mayor of the town. Jesús returned my mare to me, saying that the animal was like a second sweetheart, the first being my shotgun, and neither must be left for a moment unprotected.

The fellow had escaped from the one-cell lockup in town and was serving a five-year sentence for robbery.

Chapter V

SALENTO

The first time I ever saw a black man, I was eighteen years old. It was an extraordinary moment for me because the place I came from, the world I had known until then had left no record in my memory of any human being different from those I was accustomed to. I have no idea how old this man was. His skin looked as smooth as mine. The rest of the men were toasted by the sun, and I was the only person whose skin was still white. Jesús was cinnamon-colored, which made his green eyes stand out even more. I believe the Negro thought I was another man, because the hat I wore to shield my face from the sun and the khaki trousers belonged to Jesús. Also it wasn't customary for a woman to be traveling with a caravan of muleteers. I had seen him walk by half naked, and didn't know if he was dirty or not. Jesús told me that he was a Marmato miner and although he was already acquainted with them because he had been to Chocó, he thought it unusual that one of them should have broken away from his group. The man walked by with his head down close to my mare paying no attention to my presence. It was as though he were on lands that weren't his or, to the contrary, we had invaded his most personal territory. Jesús greeted him so that I would be able to get a look at his face, and the black man replied with an unexpected smile. His teeth flashed immediately, and my ears gradually became attuned to his voice. He had a different accent, and his hands were as huge as a five leaved silk-cotton tree. My husband asked him a few things, but all I could hear was the sound of his voice without understanding the answers. He was in fact on his way to the mines while we were headed to Salento. He said goodbye by just waving his hand and taking off.

I bathed before daybreak in a stream of icy water since I didn't like Jesús seeing me bleary-eyed. I wasn't worried about my period, because there were times before when it had not come for several months. Jesús, of course, was alarmed at first because he thought I was pregnant, and wanted to get to the new lands as soon as possible. Fortunately, it turned out to be just a delay, but the exceptions became the general rule. Eight years later my periods were finally regular again thanks to herbs that Rosario, his youngest daughter, gave me and thanks to my prayers to the Blessed Virgin Mary.

There were times when Jesús had to sit me up behind him on his horse, and I would ride clinging to his waist like a tick. The mist filtered out the sun's rays and for hours during the trek. I couldn't see Jesús right there next to me. That's how this land was. It was like floating, and, from time to time, the higher branches, like handfuls of blossoms up in the clouds, brushed our faces. The necks of the palm trees were extremely long, and disappeared into the whiteness of the sky. The land was uninhabited, and for weeks on end we didn't see a single member of our caravan. The cold of the wilderness chilled me to the bone several times, and Jesús had to revive me with a bitter potion made from cane. Frequently, I felt as though my head was going to burst, but Jesús knew the remedy for altitude sickness. At times of severest pain, I would think that I would have been better off returning to Doña Nicasia's inn, but now I no longer knew how to get back. After my muscles relaxed, I was like a sleepwalker and Jesús had to sit me up on his horse. I don't remember how many days I was in that delirious state until we reached Salento. Jesús sold part of the load of brown sugar,

leaving some for our own use. He then bought ten sacks of potatoes, and took on fresh animals because we still had many days to
go.

I cannot understand how the first people ever got to this region,
and even less how they could have stayed on. Here and there in
the desolation of those green mountain slopes, little yellow flowers
bloomed that died the following day. Then, when I was far away
from there, I discovered that the attraction lay in its bewitching
atmosphere. Nobody was conscious of the profound silence of the
landscape, the refreshing air, or the harmoniousness of the out-
lines of the mountains. We had been skirting the white mountain
peaks in the rear, and the foot of the new lands was before us. The
few inhabitants of the area lived as though they were in a paradise
that they were unable to see. They closed windows very early and
opened them at daybreak to let air in because the fog was cloaking
halters, hands, gestures, laughter, ponchos, hats, girths, stirrups,
cheese, cream, smoke, chocolate, wildflowers, berries, geese, dogs,
mules, and a white cross on the mountain.

Gradually, we were coming down from the clouds, skirting a centuries-old river of stones, and we wouldn't rest until we
had climbed another mountain. From a distance, all the different
shades of green kept on repeating, and my inner voice recognized
itself in each of the layers of colors. My hair had grown more plen-
tiful, the lines on my face more deeply etched, and my arms were
like steel. Jesús was kept busy with the drove, but made sure to
have me within sight at all times. I always helped him ferry the
pack animals, saddle the horses, treat them for insect bites, and be
at hand whenever he might need me. He treated me like a favorite
daughter.

My life was not boring because every day was different, and
time and space overlapped at a single point. My mare gave birth
before I did, and it fell to my lot to attend her delivery because
Jesús was away hunting. The poor thing's water broke before time,

and she almost died from loss of blood. Fortunately I was able to get the newborn out and save the mother's life. The first thing the mare did was to lick me, and then she cleaned her newborn. That was my introduction to how babies are born, since nobody had ever explained it to me. At that time, I still didn't really know which end was up. The only thing I prayed for was to have a good midwife at my side when my time came.

Jesús was anxious to get to our destination, and speeded up the pace. I myself had forgotten that we were headed to a specific place, not because of unconcern, but because I had lost any sense of time, and was very involved with my mare. According to Jesús's calculations, we had taken one month more than anticipated. In three weeks, we should be arriving at the hacienda, where his six children and a lot of work were waiting for us.

PART II

Chapter VI

THE HOUSE

O nce upon a time, the L shaped house that sat at the top of a hill had had doors and windows that were blackberry-colored, but it had not been painted in many years. Long before Jesús's wife died, it had fallen into a state of utter disrepair. Some rooms, like mine, had wooden floors; the others had dirt floors packed down hard as stone. The kitchen and halls, which were the most important rooms, were finished with wooden gates. Jesús had spared no effort in the installation of a wood stove made of bamboo that took up three-quarters of the area. The kitchen also had an inner window through which food was passed into the dining room, and a main door that was locked at night to keep out hungry animals. There was no chimney so smoke seeped through the cracks in the wall. The walls that separated the bedrooms as well as the façade and rear wall were made of a mixture of manure and earth. Cattle excrement was used as a building material as it solidified in the bamboo structure over the years. The house didn't require heating because the steam from the soups together with the protection of the walls of cow dung, provided sufficient warmth in rainy winter.

At first, I slept with Jesús in the same tin bed as his deceased wife, but as time went by, I arranged things so I could move to the adjoining bedroom where hoes, shovels, and pickaxes were kept. The rooms were not connected, and the entrance to mine was through a double door to the main hallway. However, Jesús knocked down part of the mud and cane wall, and visited me in the night when all I could see in the dark were his cat eyes.

Jesús's eldest child, Jesús María, was six years older than me, the second four years, and so on successively down to the youngest girl, who could have been my little sister. Bárbara, Carmen, and Rosario were the younger children who looked like their mother-they didn't bear even the slightest resemblance to their father. The third son was the one who looked most like Jesús, in the eyes as well as in his attitude toward the world. Without a doubt, the passions that linked them like twins were love of danger, horses, and women. Jesús, however, was a natural-born fighter while Israelino was a born loser.

Jesús María was suspicious of me from the first day I set foot in the house. Miguel did not see me as a mother, and treated me like another sister. Israelino tried to ignore me, but his other impulses won out. Bárbara didn't hold back a word, just to be sure to make me feel like an intruder. She did not hesitate to yell at me that Jesús would use me for a while, and when he no longer needed me, would turn me out like a stray cat. Carmen betrayed me from the start, and Rosario gave me my first lessons on how to dominate a man, even by torture, if necessary.

At first, the men took care of the cattle; the women worked in the kitchen and did the washing in the river. Jesús gradually changed after we arrived. He treated me distantly in front of his children, and was even a tyrant sometimes, but in private he was a very affectionate lover. He was away much of the time, taking his sons hunting with him. I was no longer by his side day and night like during the trek. I also missed him because now I no longer had the feeling that somebody was protecting me. On the contrary, Carmen was now the one who was with me day and night. She followed me everywhere, even to the outhouse. She had become my new shadow, and I felt watched over by her even in my dreams. One night, I realized that she was trying to eavesdrop on my conversations with Jesús because I caught her with her ear to the door. I asked her what she was doing there in the dark, and she answered that she was killing cockroaches.

It was hard for me to accept the notion of living among women because the image of femininity I had in mind was connected to my memory of Nera. Even though I knew that she was not of this world, her madness delighted me, as did her way of making up love stories around photographs. But after all, she had the time to imagine life while I enjoyed it through the parrots' banter, the slow way pregnant cows walked, the smokiness of the kitchen that made my eyes tear, and my husband's monkey smell. But I was not one of the characters in Nera's stories. I was now with women who talked women's talk, laughed like women, and stuck a knife in your back just like a man.

To get a foothold, I took over the kitchen, because if I wanted to keep Jesús's passion alive, I had better have absolute control of his diet. Bárbara and Carmen didn't oppose this, but Rosario actually helped me shuck and grind the corn. I was impressed by the naturalness with which Rosario talked about men. It was as if she had been married in former existences, and was familiar with the weaknesses of every man on earth. She counseled me on how to deal with her father, the answers I should give to make him think he was right, to discuss only certain subjects in front of him and, particularly, never to give him the feeling that I might be better on horseback than him. My stepdaughter was revealing men's secrets and it made me feel as though she were my mother. The Jesús I had known showed not the slightest sign of envy when I didn't miss once in shooting turtledoves. Quite the contrary, he laughed and gave me a hug, but with time, I learned that he was the one to measure all things, and that he tolerated certain games. The condition was never to overstep the bounds of his power.

Rosario advised on how I should treat her sisters, and the distance at which I had to keep Israelino. Her favorite brother was the eldest, and she told me to pay no attention to his glum expressions. He was always in a bad mood, and took over the duties of father when Jesús was away for long periods. Miguel paid more attention to his brother than to his father, and Israelino begrudgingly obeyed his father's orders. Jesús was pitiless with his sons, and had brought them up the way he did donkeys, by the whip. They and the third son in particular did not conceal either their own thirst for power, or how bitterly they hated their father. Jesús never for a moment held back from venting his fury on them, sometimes with a shout like whiplash, and if that did not have the desired effect, the whip he carried left its bloody marks. Out of shame, Israelino would never cry in front of me, but I sensed that he wept at night.

Jesús did not excuse the slightest mistake either in the daily chores or in the conduct of their lives. One morning while branding a cow with his initial, the animal got loose from the lasso, landing him a kick in the stomach that knocked the wind out of him. Israelino was his assistant with the job of tying up the hind legs. The boy did not follow his father's instructions on how to secure an animal, and Israelino and I nearly died because of it. Rosario ran into the kitchen where I was peeling green bananas for a stew, and between sobs grabbed hold of me by my apron, because Jesús was finishing off his son. When I got to the stable, Jesús had Israelino hanging by the feet from the hook over the scale for weighing the newborn calves, and was beating him with the fury of a river that carries along everything in its path.

"Jesús, this is the flesh of your flesh, don't you realize that?" I yelled at him in a voice so forceful that I did not recognize myself in it. "Turn him loose, or we'll both be going to the cemetery."

I was aiming the shotgun, the one that he had given me, directly at him, but he looked at me without seeing me. His eyes had that same glint as at the climax of a hunt, one that only I was able to detect. My old fellow knew that I was a dead shot, and would not think twice about doing what was necessary to stop this ritual of sadistic action. He had on countless occasions faced off others of his same ilk with bare fists, machetes, or hatchets, but never in his life had he found himself in the sights of a hunter, least of all a woman who was his own companion. The shock of seeing my shotgun barrel aiming at his forehead turned him the color of a toad's belly. Bárbara and Carmen were on their knees, each clutching on to one of Jesús's legs like flies on the paws of a bear. Jesús María looked upon the scene with hatred and contempt, and Miguel vomited in a corner.

Jesús got his horse and shotgun, took his favorite hounds, and lost himself in the mountains for three months. From that day on, Jesús María began saying good morning to me, Miguel brought in all the dry wood to be found on the road, and Israelino no longer attacked me with so much insistence. On the other hand, Bárbara and Carmen did not drop their guard. Now that their father was away, they had disconnected themselves from household chores, and paid no attention to me whatsoever since I was not their mother. Bárbara slept late, Rosario had her coffee in bed and around midday appeared in the kitchen, sniffed the pots, and told me what she had already warned me about: that, without a doubt, her father would be returning with another woman, and that my days at the hacienda were numbered. Carmen's tactics were different: she became my friend. She came to my room at night and slept at my feet. She fought with Rosario, who had already installed herself in my bed like a worm since Jesús left. I made room for them both. They told me stories in the darkness, as if I were a doll for them to play with. I sometimes cried, but they didn't notice, because they were too absorbed in the characters they were acting out.

"If you want to stay alive, you'd better leave before he gets back, because he will never forgive you for challenging him in front of us," Carmen told me.

Rosario, on he other hand, explained to me in her long lectures that her father was in love with me, and that she could see it in his eyes. I have no idea what Rosario saw, but do know that in her imagination, *she* was in love with her father. According to my stepdaughter, one of the things about me that attracted her father was precisely my daring and my sense of perspective as to what is called for in a given situation. I would never have shot another human being, except in self-defense, or for what I considered to be truth. I have no idea how these words that I had said to Jesús came out of me, but the comment about the cemetery was added to scare him, because I hadn't even seen one after I left Angelópolis. I just happened to remember the crosses scattered along the trail when we came to the new lands.

The girls ruled in the house, and the older boys tried to behave like grownups. Jesús brought potatoes and brown sugar, and they dried out the chocolate in the sun. The servants took care of the children's mother until she herself had fired them, because she believed that they were going to poison her. Bárbara had never had a boyfriend, and Carmen sneaked out at night with the farmhands. Rosario imagined having a lover, but her adoration of her father prevented her from being unfaithful to him.

How is it possible that I didn't recognize the boundless insanity of that house? I was surrounded by crazy women. But I was worse than they were, because it never entered my mind to leave Jesús. I don't blame them because if anything is inheritable, it is madness. Then, I found out that in fact Doña Virtudes, Jesús's first wife, had gone mad shortly after her husband got out of prison and returned to the hacienda. Since that time, the woman had closed herself into her bedroom with a family of flea-bitten cats. The boys had grown up by themselves because Jesús stayed away more assiduously after Doña Virtudes took sick. When she died, Jesús took the body and buried it between two yarumo trees. Only he knew where her grave was, and he never wanted her children to bring her flowers.

Chapter VII

DOÑA VIRTUDES

Everybody at the hacienda knew the reason why Doña Virtudes went off her rocker. Jesús didn't have to ask why, because he already knew from the beginning. On the very day they took her husband away to Las Delicias, a prison near Manizales, Virtudes installed Jesús's buddy, Don Eliseo, at the hacienda. The ten years of her husband's confinement had passed in a flash for Virtudes. She said it was like one second of happiness with her lover. Her eldest son was a boy of eight when Jesús disappeared from their lives, and a man the next time he saw his dad.

Don Eliseo was Jesús María's godfather and Jesús's companion on his excursions. He took care of the cattle and assumed responsibility for his new family as though it were of his own creation. The boys did not regard him as a father, but were intimidated enough by their mother to treat him with respect. The girls treated Eliseo better than they did their mother. Virtudes was jealous of her daughters' closeness to her lover. And in view of the temporary nature of her happiness, Doña Virtudes determined that nobody else had a right to share in it. She shut herself in with him for days at a time, and the only one allowed into the room was Rosario because she brought them oranges. Rosario told me that she surprised them making love on several occasions, and that they did not interrupt their sensual rituals as though she were nothing but another orange waiting to be peeled. Her mother told her that whatever she did was out of love for her children. She also said that men had to be kept satisfied at all times, or they would go looking elsewhere for a meal.

Virtudes sent her companion away when she went to fetch Jesús at the Manizales prison. She was not the same after Jesús returned to the hacienda, and soon after his arrival retired to her bedroom next to the kitchen. Rosario would go in with oranges for her mother, and spend hours talking to her. Carmen told me about it because she always had her ear to the wall, but couldn't tell what they talked about. The girl would say something and answer herself in a different tone of voice, because her mom did not utter a single word again after she shut herself in. One day I asked Rosario what the nature of their chats was, and she answered that it was women's talk.

Of the few times Carmen understood what her mother said was when she berated Jesús for taking his three male children to visit Mónica, the most beautiful girl in the town of Barcelona. Rosario had told her mother all about the visit, because Israelino described all the details of his first ejaculation. Jesús's answer to Virtudes was to ask her if she would have preferred seeing them become queers.

"Those fledglings are now of an age to be with a woman. Youngsters mount free, but I'd already paid Mónica well," Jesús told her.

The town was several leagues from the hacienda, and the closest to any vestige of civilization in those parts. More than a place for entertainment, it was an oasis for mule drivers, hunters, farmhands, and new settlers. There was so much talk about this Mónica that one day I disguised myself as a man and followed Jesús and Israelino who were very devoted clients of hers. Mónica was indeed of unusual beauty: dark-skinned, she had blue eyes, and straight Indian hair. A treasure hunter had abandoned her because, according to Rosario, she was no longer bringing him luck, and gold turned into dust every time he found any. The treasure hunter came to the conclusion that this Indian woman was protecting her ancestors. Without a doubt, she had Indian blood in her veins, but nobody objected to her ancestry or her appearance. With what she had accumulated over the years through her work, she built a pavilion enclosed with palm trees that served as a dance hall. The sawmill workers had fashioned tables for Mónica out of the broadest trunks they brought down from the mountains, and she paid for their labor with services of her own. Mónica realized that the treasure hunter had done her a big favor by abandoning her in the middle of these no-man's lands, because now she no longer had to be his slave. Her business made it possible for her to choose with whom she went to bed. Some of the women in town were saying that Mónica had fed a potion to Jesús, Israelino, Don Adán, the Mayor, Don Gregorio, the butcher, and Don Luján, the knife-grinder.

Chapter VIII

MÁRQUEZ, THE MULATTO

Jesús was twenty-five years old when he was sentenced to hard labor in Paraíso. Doña Virtudes did not utter his name in the house again, and the one time that Jesús María asked when his father was coming home, she locked him up in one of the stables. Rosario learned to repeat the story her mother told her as to the reason for her father's absence: Jesús had taken a trip to the Chocó, and was swallowed up by the jungle. Carmen, however, had a version that had filtered through the cane walls. Once she heard her mother and Don Eliseo whispering in the kitchen, and according to them, Jesús killed the mayor of Barcelona because he had him jailed for being a liberal. Some time later, I heard Mónica say that very soon after coming to Barcelona, and after the treasure hunter abandoned her, the mayor became infatuated with her. However, Mónica liked Jesús better, and could not prevent the tragedy. Jesús waited for the mayor outside her house, and they faced off with machetes. Yet Israelino had been told in Barcelona that the mayor's death was a revenge killing. It was payback for the death of his only brother. I asked the treasure hunters who stopped at the house why that happened, and they told me that the mayor and Jesús were treasure hunters together and shared many secrets.

It seems that my husband found a very big grave mound on Alto del Oso and the mayor stole the gold, and did not give Jesús a share. Jesús was not the only person who had it in for the mayor. Don Gregorio, the butcher, once congratulated me because my husband, he said, was a brave man. "Your husband has balls." And he commented without looking me in the face, "Don Jesús did us a favor many years ago: he put the mayor in his grave."

Don Gregorio was the one who slaughtered and roasted my pigs. His knife was never a millimeter off, and the animal did not suffer. Don Gregorio was also a very brave man, no doubt about it, but he was humbled by Jesús's bravery. A woman named Eva provided more details about a different version of the story. Her mother had been a washerwoman in Doña Virtudes' house, and according to Eva, Don Eliseo brought his mother, Matilde, to live at the hacienda even though Doña Virtudes was not happy with the idea of living in the same house as her lover's mother. But 'love me, love my dog', and Doña Virtudes had to grin and bear it. Doña Matilde was very friendly with Eva's mother, and Eva said that Virtudes had hatched a plan to get both the hacienda and Eliseo all to herself. Virtudes knew Jesús well, and was sure that he would defend Eliseo in a fight, no matter what. Consequently, Virtudes planned everything so that Eliseo would provoke the scuffle at Mónica's house, and the rest is history.

For one reason or another, I heard the story of what happened that evening in Barcelona from Jesús's own lips. This is it:

Jesús, his sidekick Don Eliseo, and other mule drivers had spent the night drinking and dancing in Mónica's cantina. She already had a small business set up with money she got out of the mayor. Towards morning, Eliseo got into an argument because one of the girls wouldn't go to bed with one of his friends. Jesús wanted to stop the fuss but the mayor, who was present, arrested them all and put them in the stocks. During a drunken party, it's all embraces, and all are members of the same party, but when sober, everybody is ready to die for his denomination and its heroes. Jesús was a liberal like his father and grandfather before him. The mayor belonged to the opposition party, and rivalry hovered somewhere beyond hatred. Jesús did not conceal his political convictions, and thus made many enemies in the region. The bitterest was the mayor, who just waited for an opportunity to throw him in jail. Jesús had started very young as a mule driver, and as such had arrived in the region. The new lands had no owners, and everybody who came there set himself up wherever he wished. Jesús had felled oaks, cane, and cut pathways for the animals. When the mayor arrived at Barcelona, my husband was the owner of a mountain and a hundred head of cattle.

Jesús knew from the outset that the mayor was after his land, and that he was on his black list. Jesús sent him a horse as a present when he took office, and for a time, they sat together at Mónica's house. The bad blood began when the mayor decided he wanted a beach on Rio Verde that was on Jesús's property. The incident at Mónica's house was another ploy by the mayor to flex his muscles to Jesús. The mayor put Jesús and Eliseo in the stocks, and left them in the middle of the square for a whole day without food or water. When they came out of their drunken fog, he was standing there in front of them.

"You son of a bitch," he said to Jesús, you're a disgrace to the name you bear." With that, he cracked his whip over his feet and added, "Let's see who's going to be your savior."

"Pal, take my knife, in my right-hand pocket." Jesús couldn't reach it because his hands were locked in as well as his feet.

The mayor had exposed them to public shame for disturbing the peace and endangering security. Mónica brought to bear all her influence to have them get out of the stocks, and the mayor set them free during the night.

"What a fine pair of machitos," the mayor said. "Mónica convinced me that the people would rise up against me if I don't let you go free tonight. So you can thank that little whore for my not leaving you here for at least three days."

The police opened the stocks, and Jesús threw himself like a famished ocelot on the mayor with Eliseo's knife, jabbing it into him three times, once in the throat, again in the belly, and the third time in the testicles.

Jesús never regretted killing the town's top official. For him, it was a question of honor, and that's how scores are settled between men. The day his wife went to pick him up, more out of fear than love, he had spent ten years in the prison, and he looked back at it with a hint of nostalgia. What he had missed most of the outside world were his six children and his life as a wanderer.

Chapter IX

CARMEN

Carmen was one of those women who won't chop wood and won't lend her axe. Few men were attracted to Bárbara, her older sister, but those who were sooner or later ended up being Carmen's lap dogs. That represented one more victory for her over her sister. It was nothing more than another way of humiliating her, because she had no interest in any of the suitors. What she didn't know was that Bárbara was not interested in men. Apparently, she was satisfied with just herself, inside and out. As a presence in the house she went unnoticed, except on the rare occasions when, for example, when she raised her voice to give vent to her bad temper. Her remarks were more harmful than unsweetened chocolate.

Carmen loved to make enemies. She was the general of her own army of mercenary feelings. Her sisters and I were her most detested rivals, and she spared no effort in winning out even in the most trivial discussions.

"Jesús," I would say to my husband, "get me some eucalyptus leaves. I want to steam out this plague of the chills that's invading the farm."

"Daddy," she would immediately cut in, "the best way of driving out colds is to burn plum leaves."

Well, I had gotten used to Carmen strutting with full plumage spread in front of the others, but it made me angry that she couldn't control her vanity in front of her own father. I was jealous and I admit it. And so, to retaliate against her attacks, I told him everything she did while he was away from home. Jesús told me that of his three daughters, Carmen was like a thoroughbred breeding mare. The mere scent of her attracted the males.

"A bitch in heat is what she most resembles." I once told Jesús.

I had mentioned his daughter's carryings on several times.

"My Dear," he answered, laughing, "What that young lady needs is to have her wick lit. There's no going against nature," and added, "I'll have to find her a husband."

God had bestowed great beauty on her, but forgot to supply brains. Carmen didn't know how to read and couldn't even write her name, but wasn't the least embarrassed about it. I admit that Carmen was better looking than Bárbara, Rosario and me. She has honey colored eyes, and her skin was as white as Nera's. I envied her black tresses and white teeth. I knew she cleaned them with soda ash she had her father bring her from Medellín. She was always smiling in front of the men who came to the house because she knew that her sisters would like to do the same, but were inhibited by their missing front teeth, Bárbara, particularly. She covered her mouth with her right hand when she talked. The words came out half bitten off from her vocal chords. Some time later, a quack who came by the hacienda every three months fixed my teeth and Rosario's because Bárbara didn't want any man to touch her. The old fellow claimed to be a dentist, and to prove it he would take out his box of teeth and exhibit it like a work of art. I paid him with a dozen eggs, three hens, and a sack of oranges. He thought that Bárbara, Carmen, Rosario and I spent the nights alone in my room while the men were off in the mountains. Jesús kept telling me to shut the kitchen at six o'clock and to bar my room. An oak plank fit across the middle of the inside double door. Another plank was placed at an angle against the door. Although Jesús was not particularly concerned about what might happen to us during the daytime while one on of his eternal absences, it seemed that he was indeed worried about two-legged phantoms that roamed in the night. He had told me that if I heard the geese honk at night to load my shotgun and not open the door for any reason. Geese were better guards than dogs because among other reasons, dogs snored loudly when they were dreaming, and besides, someone could poison them. Who would dare try to catch a goose in the darkness? Nobody. To keep from getting bored we sang Christmas carols even though it wasn't Christmas time. Carmen did imitations of her father, and Rosario imitated the deceased Doña Virtudes. Bárbara and I contributed the applause. We all played blind-man's bluff with Bárbara always being the one blindfolded. We would blow out the candle and hide under the bed. Bárbara could never catch us; she was so tall and clumsy. One night, we noticed that Carmen was acting very distracted, because she kept looking through the slats of the window shutters. It seemed like she was waiting for some signal.

"I have to go out and pee," she was saying, but it was hard to understand her over Rosario's squeals as she escaped Bárbara's clutches.

"I'm going to the outhouse," Carmen bellowed.

"Jesús said nobody goes out to the yard at night. Here's the potty." And I pulled the enameled receptacle out from under the bed and handed it to her.

"I'll be right back," Carmen answered, ignoring me.

Then, all at once, I heard the geese beginning to honk but didn't worry, because it was on account of Carmen being outside. When the gaggling kept on, I figured they didn't ignore her beauty even in the dark. For the long time that she remained outside, the geese kept of squawking. She came back; slamming the door in a rage, and Bárbara took off her blindfold and said, "That treasure hunter is worthless."

"Even a ghost wouldn't look at you. He came to say goodbye and that he'll be coming back for me" Carmen answered.

"High time. If he doesn't hurry, you'll take off with the first pair of pants that comes down the road."

That was the day I confirmed what Rosario had told me so many times: that her sister Carmen was carrying on with a treasure hunter, one Jesús had brought to the hacienda from Jericho.

Chapter X

JESÚS REPENTS

Several months elapsed between the threat that I made when Jesús tortured Israelino and the cat look in his eyes fixed in my memory. Contrary to Bárbara's predictions, my husband returned tame as a lamb. It wasn't to be the last time he disappeared into the mountains, and from that time on, I realized he only found rest was on a horse's back. Our trek to the new lands was just a sample of the life of the man who lay snoring at my side. I, Clara, had been the only woman in his life who really knew him very well, and he was now as attached to me as he was to his dreams.

I did not have to work at making him happy in order to please him. The joy of seeing one another after the lapse of separation was stronger than our resentments. At first it made me angry that he had left, that Bárbara would tell me he was with Mónica, that Carmen would say he was cheating on me, and that Israelino should be peeping at me from behind the stones while I was bathing in the stream. I was aware that man does not live by love alone; excluding cases like Mónica, because she loved men, even though she squeezed the last cent out of them. I envied Mónica not because she was a whore, but for being so free. The two of us had come to the new lands at the whim of men. They came and went from one mountain to another, like love-starved creatures. Mónica had attained what I had not been able to until years later: financial security. Her business was prosperous and profitable; mine required a lot of sweat and offered little return.

Well, Jesús appeared, and in his hands was a present of three hens and a rooster all dangling by their legs. I twisted the neck of one of the hens to cook him a broth, and left the other two to share the hen house with a commander in chief rooster that woke us every morning. He lost no time in exercising his prerogatives over his decimated harem, and in a matter of weeks, the well-attended hens began to populate the yard, kitchen, and stable. Before long, I was crawling under the bed looking for eggs, and Rosario looked for them on the wood floor which was a foot above the dirt floor. The hounds were the first to find them, and it was their muzzles and paws that told us with desperation where to look. I collected a hundred eggs a week on average, some of which went into the breakfast omelets, leaving the majority for me to sell in Barcelona. My earnings went into a bamboo coin bank Jesús had made for me. He told me that when I had a peso saved up I should not do what he did the time he went to Medellín de la Costa. He had his photograph taken in the park, and was left without a penny to his name. I hid my money together with Jesús's, but I knew how to write, so I marked Clara, my name, on my bamboo piggy banks. As there were no real banks in Armenia, we put the bamboo boxes full of coins under the corn stalks. Only Jesús and I knew where we had our money buried in the woods.

I began buying geese, ducks, turkeys, and guinea hens with my own money. The peacocks came later. Jesús went on clearing the land with his sons and the farmhands, and I kept adding to my flock of fowls. He asked me about how many hens there were to each rooster, and I told him that there were a lot. I finally got the number up to a hundred per rooster. I knew how many chicks each one had, how may died each season, the colors of their feathers, and who their mortal enemies were. The weasels and rats stole a lot of eggs, but with my shotgun, I managed to set reasonable limits.

Deep down, I knew that Jesús was very proud of me, although he never said so. Nevertheless, the day I told him I was going to buy the rights to the Bustamante property on the other said of Rio Verde, he took it as an affront to his manhood. As far as Jesús was concerned, I didn't need more land, and if I wanted it, he would give me some hectares, since he owned most all the mountain. Without his knowledge, I made the deal and paid the Bustamante brothers with ten bamboo piggy banks, two hundred hens and a rooster that I threw in.

On returning from another of his outings which had lasted six months this time, Jesús did not find me around the chicken coops, and Bárbara told him that I had left for good. Carmen put her arms around him and whispered in his ear that sooner or later I would take off with another man. Rosario called him into the kitchen and confessed that I was across the river waiting for him. Jesús had brought me some red-gold earrings from Marmato, which I wore for many years until one day while I was waiting for a taxi on Road Eighteen in Armenia near the Rogers workshop where they were making some metal doors for me. A man put his hand over my eyes at the same time that he addressed me by name, calling out "Doña Clara," which made me think it was some friend being playful. However, before I knew what was happening, the thief's accomplice had snatched my husband's present. I was too old by then to go chasing after a memory.

Chapter XI

THE RESTAURANT

If I wanted to have children, it was time to take more drastic measures. I was twenty six years old, and hadn't produced a child for Jesús. We tried many times, but nothing worked. When I was ready, he was sleeping too deeply to be resurrected. His frequent absences made my conceiving even more difficult. Rosario used to tell me that the best way to keep a man was by producing a son for him, so I should make it my business sooner or later to provide her with a half-brother. My poultry business kept me constantly on the go, and there was no time to be thinking about such matters. But when he came to the house drunk, Jesús would give me a hard time, saying I was good for nothing, and that I was like a mule. I had established residence in Los Alamos, and was living on the land I had bought. I left the hacienda and my stepchildren who were still there. Rosario often came to see me and would stay until Jesús got back. One afternoon, she brought me a gourd containing a concoction that she said would get me pregnant if I drank it during a waning moon. She explained that it consisted of orange blossoms, corn silk, and cactus fruit seeds dissolved in white wine. First I tried it on the rooster, and he didn't die. Then on Limber, Jesús's favorite hound. He enjoyed it so much he begged for more every morning. I had nothing to lose, so I religiously drank a dose of it right before, during, and after the waning moon. It actually worked as I got pregnant with Dionisio in less than a year. I didn't realize I was expecting until Rosario looked at me slyly one day and notified me that her first half-brother would be arriving in December. I didn't believe it, but my breasts began hurting and my feet began swelling. I asked Rosario to be godmother, and Doctor Orozco, who delivered the baby, godfather.

The birth was traumatic for both me and the infant, but with the help of pigeon broth sent to me by Mónica and delivered by one of her girls from Barcelona, I recovered. Although I lay with my legs stretched out and my body at rest, my mind was in the hen house, the pigsty, and the barn. The loss of blood in the delivery had left me anemic, and I was unable to feed the baby. Jesús hired a wet nurse, and the other servants looked after the house. The priest married us with me in bed. The notary, Don Ruperto, made out my will: my property was to go to my son and the church in Angelópolis. Jesús was to executor until Dionisio came of age. I had never seen Jesús looking so downcast and, at the same time, so happy. I don't know if he was pleased at the possibility of my death, and at having a new son for himself, or if he was depressed because he really loved me. Either way, I didn't do my step-children any favors, and got well in no time.

Jesús was crazy about our son. He spent more time with us, and less time traveling. He even stayed in Los Alamos for an entire Easter Week, a season when he usually preferred being in the wilderness to see if any flames had come from the Indian tombs. Soon after Dionisio's first birthday, when I was expecting again, Jesús went back to his wandering, but less frequently. My second pregnancy was difficult, and ended in the stillbirth of a little girl. I baptized her with the name Eloísa, after my mother, and buried her in a little white casket. With my third pregnancy, my body had become accustomed to maternity, and I even had twins. All in all, I had five males and one female to whom I gave birth at the age of forty.

The house was overflowing with children, and the presence of my husband no longer filled my sleepless nights. In addition to my poultry business, I opened a restaurant. With no time left to even brush my hair, I kept it short for years. I would tie a kerchief over my head, and have the cornmeal cakes and coffee ready at four in the morning. The fried plantains would already have been on the griddle, and the vegetables chopped for the breakfast beans and eggs. The beans were put to soak the day before to soften them. Eva, the cook, and the other servants got up at five o'clock and took my place while I went out to milk the cows. We all kept busy until seven o'clock at night when the last meals were served.

Eva had been with me since I came to Los Álamos. Clímaco, her husband, was a mule driver who would get even drunker than Jesús.

"If I get wind that you're two-timing me while I'm in Salento, you won't live to tell the tale," Clímaco warned her.

I heard him say this. The poor thing, however, was so homely that she could pass by a gang of lumberjacks without causing as much as a stir. One day, some mule drivers passing by the inn noticed her standing at the kitchen door. They stopped and one asked, "Señorita do they sell meat here?"

"Sir, this is a restaurant," answered Eva, at which the men grinned maliciously.

"Damn fools! What makes you think this inn is a butcher shop?" she snapped at them.

"Oh," one of them answered, pointing at her with his axe "we saw bones in the doorway, so we figured you were the skeleton they hung up to sell."

They had to move fast to escape the pot of boiling water Eva threw at them.

Actually, Eva was a lamentable sight. It looked like she had one eye down on her cheek and her nose stuck onto her forehead. Besides, her rear end was shriveled up from the thrashings by her husband.

The couple had two girls, a four- and a five-year old, who played with my children. Eva was a very capable woman and took charge of the kitchen when I went to Armenia on Sundays to sell the eggs and cheese. I had bought more milk cows and Jesús gave me a present of a couple of colts he had broken in himself. However, I had bought a horse at a fair in Barcelona, and learned to ride better than Jesús.

I came back from town one Sunday evening at about eight o'clock to find all the servants waiting for me at the front door of the restaurant. I didn't see Eva among them, and thought maybe she was giving birth to her third child. When I walked into the kitchen, there, on the floor, were the dogs and a pig licking blood pouring out of the lower part of Eva's body. That bastard Clímaco had stabbed a knife into her belly, and Eva bled to death. The expression on her face was one of relief, the likes of which I had never seen before on a living human. Her ugliness, however, was even heightened by the wide open eyes and the few teeth remaining that the drunken muleteer had failed to knock out of her mouth on previous occasions when he was drunk. In the end, all she could chew was a bun dunked in hot chocolate. Clímaco was caught on the outskirts of Salento trying to escape. According to what the mule drivers told me, he killed his wife because he suspected that he was not the father of the child she was carrying. Nothing could be further from the truth. Poor Eva, I could have sworn on my life as to her fidelity.

I wept for Eva like I did for my daughter Eloisa until the twins were born. Doctor Orozco had me drink an infusion of fever-few plant, and warned me to prepare for the worst. Fabio and Octavio were born each with a heart murmur. I managed to get them baptized on a silver tray and begged God on my knees not to take them away. Nevertheless, Fabio died at age three months, and I had the joy of Octavio living until he was thirteen.

I couldn't remember ever having had a sense of inner peace like that of my years at the restaurant. I had no sense of guilt about having abandoned my aunt and Antonia nor did I want to return to Angelópolis because nobody would take me in anywhere with children. Despite it being almost impossible to get news of my relatives because of the distances, I knew that my aunt had died and my sister had a string of kids. I had sent several messages with mule drivers to Antonia to come live with me, but she didn't want to leave the village. My cousin Venicia, however, accepted the offer and came to the farm with her husband.

My life was here with my children, chickens, pigs, cows, mares, my business, and the Rio Verde restaurant. By then I had taught myself not to be so afraid of my husband. Jesús was like one of his hunting dogs, happy when they caught their prey. My husband was aware that no matter how hard I tried to leave him, it was now too late for me to run away from myself.

The restaurant was like another child except that it demanded more attention than the children. Its location at the edge of the river and on a crossroads between the neighboring mountains was perfect. The engineers with their packs of mules, tents, and workers building the road to Valle del Cauca had to come through there. My restaurant became a regular stopover for lumberjacks, hunters, treasure hunters and the early colonizers of those lands.

Bathers arrived on weekends from Calarcá. Mónica rounded up her girls and brought them from Barcelona to the beach to sunbathe and get ready for their customers. Some tourists came for the fishing and others got into the water to gawk at the girls. The restaurant had its private beach and though some families brought their own victuals we never had enough and were always running out of kabobs, cornmeal cakes with cheese, meat pies, tamales, stuffing, and fritters. We would sell out, and Mónica appreciated my allowing her girls to use my beach.

There was always music on in the sunny afternoons and, in the evenings I enjoyed the books Doctor Orozco brought me from Medellín. I read very slowly because I didn't understand all the words, and when he came to examine the children for measles or chickenpox, I would get out my list of strange words and he would tell me what they meant.

Jesús couldn't read or write, but when it came to figures, he was brilliant. Mister Bremer understood about writing. He was a surveyor who was sent to this region by the government. He told how he escaped from his country during the war disguised as a Carmelite nun because they were going to arrest him. His wife and two daughters were already dead. The nuns hid him in their convent and helped him get to Spain through France. In a port by the name of Vigo he caught a ship that took him to Venezuela. I have no idea what attracted him about the place here, but he moved into a little house next to the restaurant and came there every day for his meals. I made him chicken stew and fish dishes without the fins. I prepared food that he liked. He didn't eat cracklings or pork tamales, and drank corn gruel without milk. He looked older than his age, and as though he had always been old. He was a little nearsighted and there were usually grains of rice in his beard. He had a very thick accent but was easy to understand when he spoke Spanish. He was the one who had the same kind of books as Nera, who used to keep photographs of her mother between the pages. It was *Faust* by a Johann Goethe and Mister Bremer told me that it was written in German.

Mónica once asked me if it was true that Mister Bremer read evil books. I know that Mónica had spread the rumor that Mister Bremer was a messenger of Satan because he didn't visit either her house or God's in Barcelona. Actually, he never changed his black frock coat. I believe, besides, that he did not go into the river and that is why a smell of sulphur followed him everywhere. Whenever he came into the restaurant in the afternoon, the employees ran to the kitchen holding their noses and saying, "Doña Clara, the devil is waiting for you."

Mister Bremer was not aware of his stench, and it didn't matter to me because he was a guest who paid every month on the dot and I found his conversation entertaining.

He sat up until dawn next to the light of a seven-branch candlestick reading newspapers and books that came from Europe. I would see him from the restaurant kitchen when I got up at daybreak to prepare the coffee. He would lend me some of his reading material, and give me books that arrived for him from Spain. Sometimes, he showed me maps that he spread out as though there might be gold dust in the folds. Other materials were opened with the careful hands of a midwife as he cut the string around a roll and spread out a sheet of paper on the floor like a Bedouin carpet. Some were maps of cities in the desert, others facades of Greek temples and Roman aqueducts. But the one he treated with most care and showed me as though it were his deepest secret was a map of the route of Saint James.

"Señora, I walked this route myself," he whispered to my ear. "Don't tell a soul that I am not Catholic, but I think it was the martyr Saint James who saved my life."

In fact, he traced the route with his finger, and pointed out to me all the places through which he had passed.

"It took me several months because I walked from the French border to Santiago de Campostela. My feet would split open but they were attended to on the way. I don't how I made it but I did manage to arrive alive at the saint's tomb."

Well, the truth of the matter was—I was able to verify it later—that Mister Bremer had a cousin in the diplomatic service in Bogotá. It was through this German relative in the capital that he managed to get a job with the company that was building the roads in South

America. This was how he arrived at the new lands with the engineers who opened the roadways. His task was to make a map of the Colombian Andes. This, then, was what had brought him to the new lands. There wasn't the slightest doubt about his ability, but I wasn't so sure about his purposes. On hot days, when the bathers were changing their clothes to take a dip in the river, Mister Bremer would be glued to the window for hours with his binoculars watching the girls' every little movement. One day when I said to him jokingly not to be worrying my employees, he answered that he was measuring the contours of the Rio Verde.

As time passed, we got used to Mister Bremer's presence and his smell. He was harmless and his whims hurt no one. Towards evening when there was nobody around to prepare food for, he would drop in at the restaurant to listen to the talk at a long wooden table that could accommodate thirty people. Those taking part in the story-telling sessions were milkmaids, cooks, lumberjacks, wanderers, the head waiter, his children, and mine. Jesús loved to hear the people laugh and be amazed at their anecdotes. I knew that he had spent most of his life delivering monologues. I often thought that he went up into the mountains to invent his life for himself. The dogs stretched themselves out on the floor and snoozed undisturbed by the outbursts of laughter.

Dionisio, Leonardo, and Octavio sat next to me and clung to my arms when Eva told us in a very natural way how one time she went to gather wood on the mountainside but on the way met a very handsome man who indicated the way out of the woods to her. When she held out her hand to thank him, and she noticed that the man was frozen stiff. She got home she told her mother what had happened and described the man to her mother. Her mother began to pray because she thought that it must have been her deceased husband who died when Eva was a year old.

Jesús would keep talking, repeating stories about his adventures, like the time he killed a snake because it swallowed whole calves. He told us that his grandfather groomed General Santander's white horse and that when he was a kid he had to swim across a river that was two leagues wide and was stung by a stingray. He told us how he was taught the art of prayer by an Indian in Chocó. When he wasn't able to cure the livestock with his herbs, he prayed and the cows got well. We were all equal there in the darkness and ability was measured by the capacity to tell the best stories. Jesús always won, I don't know whether it was because the servants wanted to gain his favor or because his lies were so believable that the difference between fantasy and reality no longer mattered.

His encounter with a gnome was famous in the region. He had gone one Easter Week to hunt for ancient graves with buried treasure. On the way, his horse resisted crossing a stream and stopped dead. A little naked black boy was dancing on the opposite bank. Jesús dismounted, took off his poncho, spread it out on the ground and knelt down on it. He made the sign of the cross on the poncho with his machete and asked the gnome what he wanted. The little boy smiled and went on dancing. Jesús knew that where there were gnomes there would be Indian tombs. He opened his fly, pissed in his left hand and flung it at the gnome. As a matter of fact, he had learned from the Chocó people that urine was the means of getting an evil spirit out of one's way. The little gnome disappeared, and on one Holy Saturday Jesús found an Indian grave in that same place but the gold had already been removed.

On a different note, I did indeed see the Heavenly Limelight with my own eyes. I was riding from Barcelona on my horse under a clear sky and remember taking off my kerchief because it was very hot. I was very leery of being caught by darkness before reaching home for I had once been held up and had my hand broken on the road. Nevertheless, I could see the roof of my restaurant from the hilltop and the river that looked like a silver ribbon. For a moment, I thought I was being followed and came to a stop. I looked around and heard the beating of bat wings in the custard apple tree. I drew my revolver and continued along the road. When I looked back one last time, I saw a ball of light the size of ten saucepans following me. Terrified, my horse bolted wildly. The light was so fast that it flew over my head and when I saw it in front of my horse, it divided into two smaller lights. I don't understand how I got home, but the horse took me right to my door. The next day the farmhands told me that the limelight had passed over Rio Verde. According to them, it was a mother in grief for having killed her two children and was deprived of sleep until the end of time.

Mister Brenner warned me that what I had seen was the explosion of a star Nan which, according to his calculations, was a million light years from the earth. I knew that the sun came out every day at the same time, that a waning moon was the best time to plant coffee, and that the stars in the sky did not move. The last few years, Mister Bremer spent hours observing the heavenly bodies. After the story-telling session in the restaurant, he would go out into the yard, and sit down with his binoculars. I discovered his astronomy manual among the textbooks he left behind when he took off because of the violence in the mountains. I read in it that nothing is permanent and that everything is in continuous movement.

Chapter XII

ISRAELINO

Aside from being taller than Jesús and having Doña Virtudes's white skin, Israelino was the spitting image of his father, with his same look, same gestures and voice, and same arrogance and highhandedness. He had a dozen children scattered around in Armenia, Calarcá, and Barcelona, as well as on his father's plantations. These women kept appearing at the restaurant with children in their arms to ask me for money or, sometimes, work. The only ones who stayed on at the restaurant were Horalia and her daughter, because the other four could not take the grind. Israelino lived in Caicedonia with one of Mónica's girls whom he had already gotten pregnant. Father and son had not spoken in many years. It seemed as though the poison of all mutual male hatred flowed in the veins of this father and son. However, on one May third, they came face to face.

Israelino would frequently pull up to the restaurant loaded down with whores and booze, in a late model Ford, fitted out a gramophone that blared day and night. He would roll down the window, and yell at his father saying he was a thief and murderer who had latched on to what was rightfully his inheritance from his mother. Such scenes became more frequent, and Jesús had aged without realizing it. I often had to hold him back when his rage at the insults became uncontrollable. One time I barred all the doors and threatened that if he crossed the threshold to have it out with his son, he would never see me, or the children, again. But I knew that pride would outweigh his wife's pleas. And on one May the third, he could no longer bear the humiliation of his abusive son shouting outside.

"Clara, I will not hide behind your skirts any longer," he said to me. "Once and for all, I am going out to settle scores man to man."

Although that same look came into his eyes as he would have at the start of a hunt, I was not too worried, because he did not have his shotgun at hand. This time he would be entering the ring to grab the bull by the horns. Jesús was familiar with every turn of his son's mind and to take him on was to fight himself. What was most horrifying, however, was that he saw himself as in a mirror, as a son who was a distorted image of himself. The son had destroyed himself in the effort to compete with his father. He wished to amass more hunting trophies than his father, more horses, more women and children. Even when they went to the whorehouse together, they bet on whose penis was longer. Mónica was the umpire and Jesús told me, with a victorious smile, that Israelino's was quite small.

What kept me up at night, other than the music bellowing from Israelino's car, was that he was also armed. When Jesús lifted the wooden bar off the door to face off his son, I got my pistol and locked the children in one of the rooms. As a matter of fact, I was tired of having to listen to his rants against me. According to Israelino, the old man was squandering money that belonged to him and his brother and sisters on a woman who looked like his daughter. I made no demands on Jesús inasmuch as I was able to support my family and feed all my stepchildren's children. The chicken coops, dairy farms, and restaurant had made my fortune. Mónica had rented from me the best house in Barcelona that I had bought. She had let the girls go and closed the bar. She spent her time embroidering tablecloths and making sweets for orphans. It was whispered about in town that one of the little boys she took care of at home was the son of the local priest and one of her girls. We say in these parts that usually when there is smoke, there is fire. One day when I went to collect the rent, playing dumb, I asked about the priest. Between stitches she said:

"Doña Clara, the priest is fine. He is very fond of his kid but is not giving him his name. He contributes to his support, and wants him to go to school. By the way, tell Isaraelino, your favorite step-son, to stop playing games comes up with money for his daughter, whom I am keeping here, too."

I didn't get my money slipped to me under my door, rather it represents the thousands of daybreaks I saw, and the at least million cornmeal cakes that I made in my life. My fortune was the product of continual struggle, of helping the cows give birth, of milking all the teats in the world until my hands sprouted calluses. Jesús was my man, but I was no freeloader as Israelino called me.

Well, my husband didn't realize that I was watching him when Jesús, called out to his son by his full name: "Jesús Israelino." It was raining, and his breath frosted the window on the driver's side. Israelino's words were uttered at the same slow pace as the windshield wiper. He was alone this time, his head drooping over the edge of the steering wheel. Jesús threw open the door, grabbed his son by his jacket lapels, and before his head hit the horn, Israelino, drunk as usual, managed to choke out between tears: "You son of a bitch!"

That May third, the river overflowed its banks, and washed the Ford away with Israelino asleep inside. Four days later, it was found with Israelino still inside. When he was pulled off his seat, fish and worms had eaten half his leg. Doctor Orozco saved his life, but Israelino lost his right leg. After the incident with his father, Iraelino holed up in a hut in Caicedonia where I visited him without Jesús's knowledge. He was living with a woman and her little girl.

In time, I established title for him on the properties he had there. I would go to see him even after Jesús died. He refused to use a wheelchair or to be treated like an invalid, and spent most of his time in an armchair in the living room. His lungs had also been affected by the accident, and asthma became a worse enemy than his lameness. He never asked about Jesús, and I never mentioned anything. Father and son were enemies for as long as they lived.

Chapter XIII

ROSARIO

A s for my stepdaughters, Bárbara was a spinster, Carmen went off with her treasure hunter, and Rosario married an engineer who was building the Valle road works. Rosario was the spoiled child of Jesús' first marriage. She and I practically grew up together and her clear-headedness was a constant surprise to me. Yet, as a grown woman, that gift was more sporadic. She lost her sparkle; her talk became flat and colorless, that is, until Mister Stilman appeared. I treated her more like a sister than a stepdaughter and forgave her childish jealousies. She didn't resemble her father in any way, except when they got sick, and having a cold was like the end of the world to both of them. Rosario would stay in bed, and I would bring her warm honey with lemon. Once I went to live in Los Álamos, Rosario spent more time with me, and gradually drew away from the others. Carmen said that it was a ploy of mine to turn her against them. But there was no point in doing that because they were responsible for their own estrangement. As Rosario grew, the memories of her mother began to fade like the ivory palms in the mountainside mist. Jesús had told her that if he heard her mention Virtudes's name, he would send her back to the old house with her sisters. Rosario chose to be with us, and to work in the restaurant. However, her father's restrictions drove her to resort to communicating with her mother through séances. Doña

Emperatriz Quiceno, a neighbor, owned a shop called *La Esperanza*. It was a dairy that was smaller than ours, and I rented lands to her for her cattle. I had heard that she communicated with the spirits, and one day when she came to see me, I told her that I would like to talk to my mother. She answered that first it was necessary to have a lot of faith. It was a matter of hearing what one wanted to hear, but I offered to go one night when Jesús was out hunting. Rosario, as eager as I was, ran to saddle his horse. She had already attended séances, but wanted me to confirm her hallucinations.

When we got to the dairy, all I could see was a candle flame in the center of a round table. Doña Emperatriz was slumped on a rickety stool. We sat down around her and when I asked Rosario who the others were, she put a forefinger to her lips as though to quiet a dog. At first, I didn't recognize anybody in the dark, but then I realized that Mister Bremer and Mister Stilman, the highway engineer, were secretly taking part in the séances. As Doña Emperatriz was preparing the medium, who was a man I had never seen before in the region, I wondered how a man as intelligent as Mister Bremer could let himself be taken in by a crazy old woman. But in the case of the engineer, Mr. Stilman, I suspected the reason for him being there. He had had his eye on Rosario ever since he began coming to the restaurant with the Valle road works commission, and I delivered his letters to her.

Jesús wouldn't let anybody approach his daughter. Her eyesight was so poor that I had to read Mr. Stilman's messages for her. I would also hand him the answers she dictated to me, because I didn't want him to see her poor spelling. Sometimes I had to make changes because if I put down in writing what she was telling me, he wouldn't be able to make heads or tails of it. I had taught Rosario the alphabet and arithmetic, but I wasn't much of a teacher because my pupil never learned the difference between the similar sounds of b for butter and p for putter.

Well, the medium seemed to have tuberculosis, and never stopped coughing even when a spirit took possession of his emaciated body. Doña Emperatriz was unable to call up her husband as a demonstration because the medium went into a spasm. Doña Emperatriz suspended the séance because, according to her, one of the guests had a dead person behind him. There were eight of us, and one person in the group had committed murder. Stunned and ashamed, Mister Bremer looked at me. Rosario squeezed my hand hard and fainted. I was never able to prove what was said in the dairy that night, but I always suspected that it was Doña Emperatriz herself who had poisoned her husband so that she could be with one of the farmers on the hacienda. Rosario had told me that this lad had been a trusted farm hand of Don Juan, Doña Emperatriz's husband, and that Rosario had heard her mother's voice through this farmer-medium. Doña Virtudes told everyone that she was suffering in purgatory.

Mister Stilman laughed at Rosario's foolishnesses. The two made an excellent couple, no doubt about it. I convinced Jesús that it would better if the lovers could meet in the restaurant, not at séances. The old fellow was very reluctant at first because, among other things, foreigners ought to marry their own. He assured me that this was only a fling; he knew about that class of people. However, Mister Stillman turned out to be on the level, and informed Jesús of his intentions. Rosario was not an attractive girl, but after meeting Mister Stillman, she had ordered a length of pink material and a red lipstick from Don Omar Ozman, the peddler who visited all the haciendas with the current styles in Medellin. But, what Ozman showed as the latest in Paris, Madrid, or London had been out of fashion for the last ten years. That was of little concern to me, because all I needed for work was a couple of changes of clothes. But every once in a while I'd treat myself to a length of material that was a little more elegant.

Rosario had seen a photograph in an American magazine that her suitor had showed her of an actress named Bette Davis dressed in a wedding gown. I sewed a white wedding dress for her similar to that one, and gave her a present of a wool blanket from Ecuador. Jesús got her a pair of black shoes instead of white ones since she would need them for the trip. I didn't make her a veil as long as the movie star's because I didn't have enough fabric, nor did I let her use pearls because they brought bad luck. I sent a couple of farm hands into the mountain to pick orchids for me which I combined with marjoram flowers. The bouquet didn't come out as I would have liked, but Rosario had flowers to carry in her hand that day.

I was as happy as if it were my own wedding. I sewed my outfit with my own hands. I made the dress out of two yards of emerald green silk that I kept in a closet. I had bought the material from Don Omar out of my own money. I borrowed the magazine from Mister Stilman, and considered a few different styles. Actually, the one I liked best was worn by Mary Duncan. It draped very neatly from the shoulders to a little below the knee; was sleeveless and on Duncan it fit like a dream because she was very slim. I had to make adjustments on account of my breasts being huge. The pregnancies had swelled them and my hips were a lot fuller. My height helped me out, and I didn't have varicose veins yet. So my emerald green dress disguised my bust and other bulges. I added sleeves down to the elbow and hemmed off the skirt at ankle height because Jesús would never allow me to show off one of best attributes: my legs. Although I would prefer going around the house barefoot because my feet always swell, on Rosario's wedding day, it was the first appearance for me in a pair of cream-colored shoes with heels that went with the pale straw hat. I made a flower out of a piece of material left over from the length of silk, and sewed it onto the hat. I also wore gloves the same shade as the shoes, but I took them off after the ceremony in the church in Barcelona to take charge of the wedding feast. I folded my emerald green dress, wrapped it in tissue paper Mister Bremer had given me for covering books, and put it away with a few moth balls in a burlap sack. I never wore it or put the new shoes on again. They made my every last bunion ache.

I prepared a hundred chicken and pork tamales. And chicken broth and cornmeal cakes for the late-nighters were not lacking. My dear friend Maria Torres prepared the cake and sweets in Calarcá because I didn't know anything about desserts. Jesús roasted three suckling pigs and hired musicians. The celebration lasted three days, and the guests had to be thrown out at the end.

When her husband the engineer finished the section of highway in the region, he took Rosario to Buenaventura. From there, they got on a boat to Perú and then Chile, from where she wrote me letters telling about their new life. Jesús was downcast for a few days, but got over it, and was happy as a lark again. The old fellow celebrated his daughter's trip with another roast suckling pig and drinks for all the farmers. Rosario was his connection to the ghost of Virtudes and with her departure he cut off the few ties remaining of his previous family.

The two of them were crazy in love, but Rosario didn't like separating from her father, and even less leaving the country. She was more stubborn than an old mare, but I persuaded her her by telling by that a foreigner would treat her better than one of our own countrymen. Mister Stilman neither smoked nor drank, and it seems that she was his first sweetheart.

"My dear," I kept telling her day after day, "don't be a foolish girl. You couldn't get yourself one like this, even made to order. So stop the nonsense and go with him."

Rosario didn't have to be gulping down orange blossom tea like me in order to get pregnant. In Valparaíso, she had twins who looked like their father, with the same calm personality as their mother. The government of Chile gave her husband a steady job building roads in the provinces. The nature of his job kept him away from home much of the time, leaving Rosario alone for long periods. She commented in her misspelled letters that she believed her husband was seeing another woman because when he came home, he was overly attentive to her. Mister Stilman had a jawbone like a mule's although his blue eyes gave him an angelical appearance. His body odor smelled like sour milk, and he sweated even when he bathed at night. Rosario had told me that, but I paid no attention to her nonsense.

Mister Stilman was so ugly that not even Mónica's girls, who don't pass up a single sinner on the streets of Barcelona, would ask him what time it was if they saw him coming. Poor fellow! God was pitiless and vented his entire divine wrath on him.

And how!

When I saw him at Doña Emperatriz's séance, I thought the American was ugly as sin. For that reason and other details I'm too embarrassed to mention, I can't imagine any woman other than a wife who would venture to go to bed with him. His ugliness didn't bother Rosario but, on the contrary, she saw him as resembling the image of the Savior that hung in the living room, in profile with a very straight nose and blonde hair down to the shoulders. His mustache was clipped close by a barber's scissors and did not look like the brush strokes of an anonymous artist. His beard was thicker and cleaner than Mister Bremer's.

Jesús Christ's white face and muscular neck, inspired by the artist's imagination, corresponded to no denizen of these parts. It was apparent that the artist had taken pains to make him look familiar. Our Savior appeared to have recently bathed and put on cologne ready to ride his horse and travel the world. The glance from one blue eye was directed toward the right side of the gilt frame. It made no difference in what direction one moved in the room, that blank look followed you to every corner. Jesús had brought me the painting from one of his trips because a priest had to make payment on a house for one of his mistresses. The picture of the Savior, which he used to pay Jesús what he still owed him, had decorated the sacristy of his convent. I wanted to return it to the convent, but my husband wouldn't let me.

"That Savior is not leaving this house, because this is holy ground, too," Jesús yelled at me.

And so I wrote back in my letters that Mister Stilman was a saint, and that she should thank the Lord for not having a husband like mine, who would have a go at anything that moves as long as it was wearing a skirt. Rosario devoted her time to her daughters, the house, and her jealousies. I answered her one time that having a husband who was always off somewhere had its advantages, because his homecoming was always an occasion to celebrate.

Chapter XIV

PACHA

In those days, Pacha was the best known fortune teller in Armenia. She was living in the Santander neighborhood, and even though I put no stock in the tall tales of a crazy old lady, I went to see her. She told me to cut the cards into four piles, then shuffled them together and had me cut the deck again. I went along with Doña Pacha, because I enjoyed watching how nimbly she moved her hands. I don't know what I was doing there, and much less liked having to pay her to tell me a bunch of lies. Pacha studied the cards carefully, and without looking at me, asked if I had a mourning dress ready. I had buried three children, stillborn Eloisa and the twins, little Fabio and Octavio. The black clothes brought back unhappy memories. I had even given away the most expensive ones, of silk, to the servants. Yet it made me furious that this old woman should be telling me that somebody close to me was going to die. The kind of predictions people went to hear are of a good business deal, or where they might find a buried treasure because the dead one was making noise and keeping people awake. I always told our cooks that the reason the ladles rattled in kitchen was because we had rats the size of racoons. I had seen them myself.

Although I resented having to pay for a visit to be scared out of my wits, I would rather bury ten husbands than one of my children.

I found it hard to believe that Providence would want to take away another child of mine. I loved all my kids, but had felt something special for one of them, Octavio. He was very affectionate, mimicked his father, and tried to find order in his world of his siblings and his dogs. Octavio was the twin who survived birth after my shock at Eva's misfortune. His heart gave out, though, when he reached thirteen. Octavio was blond, had blue eyes and a melancholy expression that reminded me of my father. Every moment of his life was devoted to me. I spent the greater part of my time in the kitchen and he was my most faithful companion. From the time he had learned to walk, he was at my heels. At four in the morning, he would get up with me, and I would let him help me. I could feel him observing my every movement, gesture, and step. Occasionally, he would keep quiet for long spells while I was milking, and he would receive a reward of a glass of warm milk. The two of us looked after one another. I would keep an eye on him from the kitchen windows while he was bathing in the river with the mutts. He would spend hours in the water till his lips turned blue. On the day that Doctor Orozco detected the first symptoms of his asthma, I felt as though the world had swallowed me up. It was just a matter of time, and Octavio understood that that he didn't have long. Jesús had a number of children, but I had only one like Octavio. Octavio's death depressed the old man because it made him aware of his own mortality. He still kept the boy's patent leather shoes in a chest together with the dried flowers of his funeral. That my other children were different, I was able to verify later on.

Well Pacha was right. Three days later, a driver brought me the news from Caicedonia: Jesús had collapsed in the street and lay there *per omnia saecula seculorum*. Doctor Orozco's office was in that town, and he was his doctor, too. He had forbidden him from drinking alcohol and eating cracklings. Jesús paid no attention to anybody, and said he would rather die than give up his fritters. I was convinced that he would trade me for a dish of pig's feet with cabbage and beans. No doubt about it, the doctor's prognosis and Pacha's prediction put him in his grave. Jesús died of a heart attack on his way out of a medical checkup. He suffered no more than a chest pain and death throes that lasted a second. He always said that this was the way he wanted to die, not rotting in a bed. Fortunately, he had been to the notary that very day to sign over to me two blocks of houses he owned that bordered on the town square. When Jesús died, the mountain and other properties were divided among his six heirs and my kids. My children and I inherited *La Primavera* where the dairy farms were. As for me, my own fortune had grown thanks to my work and my savings.

By 1949, we had moved into a yellow house in the Berlin section of Armenia. The restaurant was no longer as profitable as it used to be because we had moved to Armenia for safety reasons. I wasn't able to tend to it on a regular basis and a manager was now taking charge of the restaurant and Los Álamos.

Mister Bremer had to leave the little house next door, and arranged to be sent to Argentina on another expedition. I received occasional letters from him in which he reported that he was living with relatives in Buenos Aires.

News of the death of the important Liberal politician Jorge Eliécer Gaitán did not reach the region until days after his assassination in the capital on April 9, 1948. We Liberals had to leave the farms on which we reared our children. Jesús didn't live to see the mutilated corpses floating by on the river, or the piles of the dead in the squares of Córdoba, Pijao and Barcelona. The old man had warned again and again that things were going to get very rough for Liberals, and convinced me that we should move to Armenia, particularly for the safety of the children. Some police troops had come to the region, and I rented several of my houses in Barcelona to them as offices for the Cisneros Battalion.

I realized that with Jesús gone, I didn't have a single ally anymore to protect my interests. I needed the old man because among other reasons, as a widow with four children, and as a property owner, I would be considered fair game. That's what may have been thought, but I had no intention of remarrying. When he was alive, whenever Jesús wasn't around, and off for a long spell, I would hang out a wet pair of his pants. I noticed that outsiders seeing trousers on the clothesline would behave respectfully towards me. If I had any reason to be distrustful, I would say that my husband was on his way back from the coffee patch. But now Jesús was no more than an idea in my imagination, and I had only my shotgun and gumption to protect me.

The first decision I made was to close down the poultry operation and leave a skeleton crew on the farms. Several of my farm hands had already been killed, and some of the properties were abandoned. In La Primavera, for instance, the only watchmen on alert were hunting dogs and the geese. I used to arrive unannounced, and I would leave food for them in the yard, and change the water in the basin for the ducks. There were always dead animals in the corridors, and some had been stolen. I felt as though I was sneaking into my own property, but it was a practical way of survival in the midst of this kind of warfare. One time, while I was feeding the chickens, a band of some forty strong appeared with broken carbines slung across their backs. I recognized various faces of farm hands who had worked in the dairies, and some who had been customers at the restaurant. Others were the children of farm administrators. Their fathers had been killed, and they survived by hiding among the coffee bushes. They were barefoot and sweating. They greeted me by my name, "Good day, Doña Clara."

"Good day, gentlemen, what can I do for you?"

"Could you let us spend the night in your stables?" one of them asked, a fellow with a face like a pineapple, covered with the scars of neglected measles scabs.

"Of course," I answered without a moment's hesitation.

I opened the kitchen, killed chickens and cooked them a stew. I didn't ask them their politics, and they knew mine.

"Well, now, Doña Clara," pineapple face went on, "would it be okay if we took a few steers?"

"Sure, whatever you need," I answered with a not very ready smile.

They never laid a finger on me, nor insinuated that they might. I think they admired me for being one of the few who had not abandoned their lands. It was like walking on eggshells, and seemed like it would cost your life if you said a wrong word.

It was just as well that Jesús didn't live to see his horses running loose on the dry fields with no food or attention. Many houses were torched; mine were no exception. When Mónica notified me that Los Álamos was on fire, it was already too late. The mud and bamboo house went up in flames like paper, leaving nothing standing but the bare lignum vitae trunks. Among the ashes of the restaurant, I found a small bag that had escaped the fire, because it lay underneath a stone corn hopper. On handling the bag, the yellowed cloth broke open, a white powder spilled out, and disappeared into the cracks of the wooden floor, and I was left holding in my hands the bones of another hand. Other bones fell on the ground, turning into powder, as well. The closest experience I had had to seeing a mutilated hand was the time I had watched Jesús gnaw on a monkey's paw. I paid no attention to the chatter of the kitchen maids, but evidently these remains had been there for many years. They claimed that somebody who had done an evil deed was jinxing the place. But then I began to wonder, because I had the evidence right in my hands. In general, I never thought of one really having bad luck or good luck. That would be giving too much credit to fate. One was responsible for the embittering or sweetening of one's own life. I had chosen to go with what suited me. I didn't hear footsteps in the night, or spoons rattling around in kitchen drawers, like the rest of the staff did. I would say the Lord's Prayer, just in case, to save Eva's soul from torment.

So it went. Evil eye or whatever, Armenia was the safest place to live in because there was always a curfew at nightfall. And so I went from an outdoor life to a city that had barely one main street as long as Barcelona's. The windows and doors to the house were kept shut, and conversation was in whispers. Jesús could never have stood a secluded existence, much less in a house full of children. His heart attack kept him from getting about very much in the corridors of our house in the Berlin neighborhood. The time a pair of ruffians assaulted him in front of the house he was very tipsy and didn't even know what had happened to him. While he was alive, I wouldn't turn in until he got home. Once I heard sounds outside, close to the hydrangea near the window, I looked through a small window, and saw two thugs grabbing at my husband. I ran out waving my revolver and fired into the air. They stole his hat and a small pouch he was carrying, but the next day he didn't remember a thing.

PART III

Chapter XV

BERLIN

Berlin was the upscale neighborhood of Armenia. Many of us who fled the countryside had settled there. Getting to Berlin required scaling what was practically a mountain because the houses were all built on the heights. Access in the winter was as impossible for cars as animals, which would fall in the flooded streets. Some settled in Berlin for the same reasons we did, like the Tarquino family, for example, which consisted of the boss man himself, the mother, and a herd of twelve children. Class distinction was unknown because all had common roots, and fear was the unifying factor like inside a cave. It wasn't until my eldest son had returned from the seminary with different ideas that the stability of the neighborhood was threatened.

There were twelve children in the Tarquino family. Don Pedro argued with his daughters all the time, and was strict with the boys. The older girls were my children's playmates, and when I had to go to La Primavera, they would stay in the house and babysit my youngest daughter. I treated them as my own children, and they would tell me everything Dionisio had done when I was away. The girls attended the Official Girls School and the boys The Rufino. From the rear window of my house I could see them parade in their white uniforms along the Camino del Navegante which during rainy spells became the only open passageway for pedestrians in the neighborhood. The girls left at six in the morning, came home for lunch, and returned to school. One time when I asked Estelita how long a walk it was there and back, she answered offhandedly: an hour. I was amazed at how clean those Tarquino girls managed to keep in all that mud. Doña Inés, the mother, did not excuse a speck of dirt on their shoes, to say nothing of the wood floors which those same girls scrubbed and waxed every single night. Dionisio had repaired a broken down phonograph. However, playing music in the house was forbidden because it was associated with places like Mónica's. Jesús brought back a phonograph and a big mirror on one of his trips. He swapped two sacks of brown-sugar loaf for them with a dealer who handled goods from Medellin. Well, the old guy lost no time in buying records and would play one for me every time he got drunk. His favorite went: "You no good no more, doing' what a woman good for..." I was getting fed up with that rhyme of his and his mockery. One night he came to the restaurant soused to the gills and turned on the phonograph, I jumped out of bed in a fury and threw the speaker into the river and hit him in the head with the records. I don't know how I missed really injuring him. I didn't talk to him for days and to make up, he brought me another Spanish shawl and one of his sows that was about to have a litter.

I had been keeping the gramophone as a trophy of one of my battles. It didn't play until Dionisio got to work on it. He built a speaker and attached it to the machine. He organized free parties at home in the afternoons with sodas and meat patties to which all the Tarquinos and other neighbors were invited. Afterwards, when I returned from the farms, exhausted, the girls would fill me in me with all the details of the celebration to which I had not been invited.

The Tarquinos told me that Dionisio kept on mourning Jesús for months after his death. He would bring all the children together in the living room, give them dahlias that he picked in the fields and have them file past a metal box. He sang the songs and absolute silence was observed. I had become aware many years earlier of my son's musical talents. Don Omar Ozman, the peddler, who came by Los Alamos every three months, had mentioned to me that Dionisio had all the earmarks of a minstrel because from the time he was a small boy he would memorize entire conversations and then repeat them turned into songs. I took that as an insult and stopped buying trinkets from the Turk. No question, however, that my son could have the finest voice and piano teachers if that was what he wanted.

What really troubled me was the empty space Jesús' passing left in the lives of the two older boys. Dionisio was fifteen and Leonardo a year younger. It didn't matter that much to the other two. I put Dionisio in the seminary in the capital because he would be safe there and if, later on, the priesthood wasn't for him, he could devote himself to becoming a singer. At the seminary, he could learn Latin, Greek, and even German. I was able to offer them nothing but encouragement and financial support and lived, myself, in constant dread that we could all be killed at any given moment I wanted my children, at least, to survive. Little by little I got them each enrolled in their respective boarding schools, the boys turned over to the Marists and the younger daughter to the nuns of the Presentation who would look after her. I didn't want them exposed to the kind of horror I had seen in the eyes of orphans whose parents had been hacked to pieces as they looked on, mothers left widowed and unable to speak, the haggard faces of men destroying one another.

Chapter XVI

THE SQUATTERS

Bellavista was one of the largest of the farms I inherited from my husband. We had worked shoulder to shoulder on that mountain, Jesús and I. We planted Arabica and Robusta coffee to which we had to carry very large bamboo tanks full of water because of a drought that lasted four months, and we also had to plant shade trees to protect the coffee bushes. We had over two hundred milk cows as well as horses in the stables, and at harvest time at least five hundred men picking the coffee berries by hand. By 1963, Bellavista had been taken over by the squatters. Forty families moved into my property, and did not leave until such time as they had sold their small parcels to my enemies interested in that land.

In view of the violence in the region, I had to give up regular visits not only to La Primavera and Los Alamos, but to Bellavista as well. My neighbors recommended not returning to the mountain until things had simmered down. Some of our friends left for Cali and Bogotá and others went abroad with their children. But this was my place, and I wasn't about to waste my time complaining. In any case, I tried to maintain a healthy environment for my children but at the same time, it was impossible to insulate my Leonardo from those sinister scenes. He had witnessed the execution of the manager of Bellavista. The riffraff made a surprise appearance on the farm, tied up all the farmers, and shot him in front of them and his wife. Leonardo overheard one of the murderers say, "He had it coming, the snitch."

My son spent the night at the farm. He had intended to take a sack of coffee early the next morning to sell at Señor Arango's warehouse, but when he heard the shots, he sneaked out through the coffee plantation. He arrived at Armenia looking like he had escaped the clutches of the devil. He was only seventeen at the time and the look in his eyes seemed to indicate that he had changed forever. The only time he smiled now was when he looked at a woman. I was even more frightened when he shot and killed the dog because it was eating up the eggs. It was as though he was sharpening his aim for bigger game. It distressed me to see the venom in those green eyes, for I realized that it was only a matter of time before he would be taking it out on his own kind. Although he obeyed me meek as a lamb, he was pitiless towards his workers. He was infallible in anticipating danger, a desirable trait in the turmoil of our uneasy world. It was best to be prepared for any attack. I didn't care for his friends, and disliked his women even more. He fathered his first child when he was eighteen and still unmarried. Leonardo grew up fast and was quite at home in a world of chaos. It upset me to observe that he had skipped adolescence and turned overnight into a hardened adult. Also his character was so very flawed that I found it hard to attribute this to a failing on my part. I knew my eldest son Dionisio inside and out; not so difficult, after all, to know somebody who says everything he's thinking. But Leonardo destroyed his victims, leaving not the slightest clue. Unfortunately, I never knew who those victims were, but was aware of his heavy breathing and long periods of silence. My intuition told me that he was playing according to the rules laid down by the Era of Violence, but I never dared question him as to the when, where, or how of his deadly affairs.

On one evening that seemed overly quiet, I wasn't able to get any closer than a few kilometers from the main entrance to the Bellavista hacienda because that was far as my driver could go. I had a load of corn for the animals, and a revolver in my pocket. There were several men with red flags on the turnoff road. It was closed because overnight the mountain had been transformed into community property. The slogan was "*The land belongs not to the owners but to those who work it.*" That's what it said on their banners and that's what the peasants were shouting.

Their shacks were scattered all along the road, some were made of bamboo, some were covered with banana leaves, and a few with rags and torn burlap sacks. Only one was roofed with sheets of plastic that I recognized as table cloths from my dining room. It was a cemetery for the living, not the foundation of a settlement. I got out of the pickup with my hand on my revolver, which I always kept in my pocket. One man wearing a mask, apparently the leader, approached, tipped his hat, held out his hand, and greeted me as though we knew each other. I did not take his hand, but he ignored my rejection as something not unexpected. I noticed that his hair was thin and that he smelled very bad.

"Doña Clara, You'd better go home to your house on Avenida Bolivar. This is no place for a lady like you."

"Who are you?" I asked my hand in my pocket, finger on the trigger.

"That doesn't matter. We are now the owners of this mountain. You've abandoned it and, what's more, you don't need it. We know you have other haciendas and will not be left destitute. We want this land and must have it so we can feed our children."

The few dogs left at the Bellavista house ran over to me, wagging their tails and frisking about. Apparently, they were the only living creatures left to greet me. Bambina, a young bitch that was good for nothing but having puppies, peed with happiness when she saw me.

"Doña Clara," the leader of the squatters said, "this little animal now lives with us. She is very grateful and eats everything."

I must admit that the man talking to me had been very well trained. He was well spoken and respectful. His amiability caused me more uneasiness than his mask and the shotgun slung over his shoulder. He was very sure of himself on this territory that did not belong to him.

"Look here, I'm not interested in playing games. What is it you people want?"

"The land."

In the first place, I could not get it through my head that I wasn't able to set foot on my own property because some filthy paupers were blocking the road. Secondly, what did those sons of bitches think? That there was no law to stop them? But, I was very much mistaken, because the squatters were protected by the law. In fact, it was not a matter of some miserable rabble all of a sudden deciding from one day to the next to take possession of a mountain. The defiant attitudes of those masked figures that gathered around to face me indicated that they were ready to attack or defend themselves, if need be, with stones. The faces of those individuals were covered with black cloths and paper bags with eyeholes. Why didn't they stand up like men and show their faces? I was a woman and alone. There were ten of them, and I, alone, was standing up to them. Sure, they were more scared than I was. But in a gang they were dangerous and wouldn't hesitate to wipe me out.

I talked it over right away with an army colonel who gave me an immediate answer, "Take care, Clara. They're Communists. We are going to militarize the region, and you mustn't show yourself around there. We planted a few agents among the squatters, and according to their information, your life is in danger."

"Look here, if you think I'm going to pee in my drawers and hide like an armadillo, you're very much mistaken. No Communist is going to scare me."

Actually, it wasn't the Communists I was afraid of. Rather, I suspected me the Conservatives on the borders of Bellavista. It wouldn't surprise me if they were after these properties themselves and were in cahoots with their gang of hired murderers, inciting them to carry out blood baths. They had assassinated many liberals in the region.

However, according to information obtained by the Colonel, the invasion of the squatters had been organized from Bogotá. When the peasants planted their flags on Bellavista territory, they were very sure that the government would cede them that land.

Through my connections, I was able to have some soldiers from the Eighth Brigade sent to put the area under military control. That way, I was able to take out some of my things at Bellavista. And I found myself obliged to resort to lawyers. The legal channel was the only one open to me for getting my land back. Unfortunately, I was in their clutches for quite a while, feeding fourteen lawyers over a stretch of five years. I hired them all at the same time, and paid them high fees, but none were effective. It was hard to tell which of them was the most ignorant. They themselves couldn't agree on anything, and had turned the case into a rhetorical jumble. They were unfamiliar with the legal procedures involved, and the only advice they could give me was to write off Bellavista and leave it to the squatters. The government would deal with me. I think that rather than defend me, most of them became my worst enemies. In short, they double-crossed me, some out of cowardice, and others because they were scoundrels. The organizers of the seizure of Bellavista threatened several of my lawyers and the others could be bought off cheap.

My chief lawyer, Doctor Arcila, had his office in Calarcá, next to the Coffee Bank. He was recommended to me by my friend Obdulio Barrios, for whom he had recovered some stolen cattle. From his uncurtained windows, one could see the lottery-ticket sellers and candy peddlers in Bolívar square. On his desk there were always disorderly piles of papers and two ashtrays filled with *Pielroja* cigarette butts. On the wall, there was a diploma from the *Universidad Externa de Colombia,* a certificate from a course in México, and a photograph of him shaking hands with former President Laureano Gómez.

I didn't care so much about his being a Conservative, but the fact that he was bald and limped was very suspicious and set me to thinking. My instinct wasn't far off. I soon found out that his brother had a hacienda bordering on mine at Bellavista. Doctor Arcila was interested in my losing my land because, among other things, his brother–or he himself–would then be able to buy up the land from the squatters for peanuts.

The squatters' lawyers bribed a number of my lawyers. Every legal step I took to obtain an eviction order was denied by the judges because the squatters were already informed of my plans. Nonetheless, I wasn't just sitting back waiting. I stayed up late all night reading and analyzing the new regulations concerning land distribution.

How could they expropriate Bellavista just on the basis that there was a law saying so? Who were the ones really behind this case? What would they do with the land? The idea was to divide the loaf among the poor and in the eyes of the state, I was a landowner. But wasn't I also one of them? Who was it who always had a plate of beans ready for those peons now against me? I, Doña Clara, eased the hunger pangs and slaked the thirst of lots of families because I knew what it meant not to have an egg to eat more than once a year. My stomach, too, had suffered the agony of poverty. At the same time, I sweated blood clearing these impenetrable forests. Jesús felled walnut trees, discovered springs, bored wells, and ransacked every square inch of that mountain for gold. But he didn't notice that he had himself changed the nature of that absurd place forever. How sad! The old man died without ever realizing that Bellavista mountain was the real treasure.

My shysters accused the squatters of being Communist fifth columnists. The agrarian reform considered them the dispossessed and, on the other side, us, the cruel owners of thousands of hectares who were getting rich off the sweat of others. The state considered a duty to distribute the land among the peasants for the good of the country and its progress.

I did not see myself as on the other side of the fence, that is, as a villain who grabbed land I had no right to. I spoke the same language as that rabble who was threatening to kill me. Anonymous messages came under my door telling me to get the troops out of Bellavista or they would decapitate me. They tried every kind of intimidation in the book, calling constantly on the telephone to insult me. The voices were anonymous, but I recognized all the squatter faces. They never looked me in the eye, but I knew the history of every one of them. Many had been coffee pickers on the hacienda, and I was present at the births of many others because Dr. Orozco couldn't get there in time. I had cut the umbilical cord of lots of the others who later grew up to work for me. I saved the lives of a good number of those children.

I was not about to retreat a single step. I made inquiries on my own, and hired a Communist attorney in Bogotá, Doctor Alfonso Romero Buj. You fight fire with fire and who better in this case than one of their own? Alfonso had a good reputation among his enemies as well as his friends. Actually, the Communists weren't all that bad. Doctor Alfonso's wife, Nidia, was very pretty; slim, with wavy black hair. I don't know how she managed to be so elegant because she had a newborn and two other young children. Alfonso and Nidia became my adopted children because they had spent long periods in Armenia. I put them up in the Hotel Atlántico. When my daughter Marta María had her third child, they gave her a present of a blue carriage. They were bored by the cold, and besides, Nidia hated politics. I advised Alfonso to pay more attention to his wife, and not to leave her alone for so long. According to him, though, his work in other cities and trips abroad obliged him to be away. Some time later, Alfonso confirmed to me what had come out in the newspaper: Nidia had abandoned the family and ran off with a Venezuelan revolutionary.

After that, Alfonso arranged an appointment for me with the Attorney General of Colombia. Due to the lawyer's influence and, particularly, a letter I sent the distinguished Attorney, we succeeded in having this representative of the national government receive us in his office. Alfonso accompanied me to the appointment. I showed the Attorney General the deed that authenticated my ownership of the property. He accepted the document and as he read in silence, my lawyer read it aloud.

"In the city of Armenia, notarial circuit of the same name, Department of Caldas, Republic of Colombia, in my presence, Gonzalo Toro Patiño, second notary of the circuit, and before the witnesses...I certify that Señora Clara de Márquez, with whom I am personally acquainted, is the owner of a regional farm under the name 'BELLAVISTA', located in 'RIO VERDE' district of the township of Calarcá. The property is registered by deed number one thousand one hundred and ninety-one (1,191) on the seventeenth (17th) of July one thousand nine hundred and fifty-seven (1957) ..."

"Don't read on, Dr. Romero," said the Attorney General, "I also know how to, read, and quite well."

There was no doubt as to my being the owner of Bellavista. And so, I proposed, because I did not want the lawyer to be speaking for me, that if the state was interested in protecting all its citizens, I was willing to sell the property to the government. After five years of litigation and negotiation, the Office of the Attorney General sided with me, and the government paid a much lower price for Bellavista than its real value. The state bought the hacienda of Bellavista from me, divided up the land into parcels and issued deeds to the tiny lots for the squatters. After completion of the agrarian reform, the peasants sold their lots to others because of political pressure, plain greed, or because they weren't able to farm the land because they had no money at all. Everybody lost: the state, the squatters, and my family.

Chapter XVII

MY SELF-DEFENSE

Iwrote a letter to the Attorney General and my Communist lawyer corrected it for me. This is a copy of the letter to the Attorney General of Colombia which he received before we met in his office in Bogotá.

"How much longer, distinguished Señor Attorney General, are the squatters at Bellavista going to try your patience and mine? To what extremes are we to be driven by an audacity as boundless as this? Do those driven people, by any chance, fear the law of God or of man? Are they not alarmed by the day and night army surveillance, the words of the Governor or the Archbishop? Do they not realize that our fate has been cast and that our good name and that of our nation will sink into failure if an agreement is not reached? Mr. Attorney General, do you not understand that we all know their intentions? Do you think I do not know that the squatters have sent you a letter and insist that I surrender Bellavista into their hands?

Some of the plotters have convinced many people that Bellavista produces nothing because I do not sow the soil. Yes, of course, I had to abandon that mountain because the conservative mob was going to kill me, just as they murdered some of my liberal administrators.

Señor Attorney General, if you lived in these mountains you would be a witness to the mutilated corpses that are washed down by the rivers. Don't believe that I left the mountain because I don't need it, and I have other properties. They forced me to leave my own land. In the name of the parties, our soil has become saturated with the smell of death. If I have managed to survive all these years of violence it is because I have friends in all places. I am not the leader of any party and I do not sponsor candidates or warlords in the region. I have never exploited my farm hands. I've paid them good salaries, taken them to the doctor when necessary, dressed them when they had nothing and eaten with them. I get confused when they call me a landlord, because this is the first time I have heard this word applied to me. I am treated with contempt and distrust because I do not allow my lands to be taken from me. For God's sake, what times we live in! What customs! What impudence!

The governor is aware of this, some senators, too, and the case has even reached the ears of *Señor Presidente*. But the squatters are still there, and I have to ask permission to enter my own properties. I am even afraid that my life and that of my family is at stake. How would you feel if one afternoon you came home and could not even enter the garden because some strangers were now living in your house? What would you think? That you went to the wrong address or that you're crazy? How would you act if, besides taking away your home, you were threatened and had to leave, with all due respect, with your tail between your legs? What times we live in! It's as if the birds were shooting at the guns.

And we, the citizens, believe that the representatives of the State must prevent the consequences of envy, partisan hatred, and the tricks of the so-called Communists! The enemy lives with us and tries to do away with the little sanity that we still have by using a rifle pointed at our heads. Among what sort of people are we? What kind of towns are we living in? What type of a republic do we have? I understand nothing about Communism. However, word is out that behind the Communists are public traitors who have an unbound ambition for these lands. Those people who today pressure the squatters so that they rise against the nation are the same ones who have sown terror among the peasants and owners. Among the fourteen attorneys that defend me in this never-ending feud, I have a few loyal ones. Everything comes to light, Señor Attorney General! Some have informed me that they even have the names of the conservatives that have already sent in their offer to buy the the small parcels of land. I have no doubts about the good intentions of the government, but you must not close your eyes and fail to see the enemies who want to get rich treading on the backs of the peasants and people like me.

I know I am the target of the attacks of those people who call themselves the defenders of the laborers. But don't you know that I am also a peasant without land, another person expropriated from the mountain? I am a simple, humble woman. I didn't get an education at school, and everything I learned was in the University of Life. I also didn't have parents, riches and luxury in either my childhood or youth. What poverty are these barefoot people talking about? I also know what misery and abandonment are. And those same men who have nothing today accuse me of being a landowner, of usurping their land, of stealing bread from their mouths. But is it possible that they deny the fact that, because they are unfortunate, they have a divine right to kindness? That because they are poor they have a good heart? I know what corrupt thoughts come to mind when a stomach is empty. Don't try to fool me! Resentment and envy are not feelings exclusively of the powerful, but are hidden in the souls of all Christians.

Is it necessary to wait longer, Señor Attorney General? You have the power to decide the future of these unfortunate families and my own hopelessness. You can free me of great dread when I enter your office or you can tell me to my face that I have no right to reclaim this land because the laws say so. Neither they nor I will suffer when, with your magnanimous power, you authorize the purchase of these lands and pay me for the drops of blood and the tears that I spilled when I wrested fruits from this mountain.

I, too, am a Colombian citizen and, as such, I follow the laws of this nation. I have paid my taxes; I have given donations to the church, to orphanages, to retirement homes, hospitals and jails.

Señor Attorney General, justice is in your hands. I am merely a widow with children and an anguished citizen pleading for your help.

Your servant,

Clara de Márquez
Citizenship ID number 4,442,694
Issued in Armenia, Caldas".

Chapter XVIII

POLANCHO

The government bought the hacienda through the Colombian Institute of Agrarian Reform. Years later I went through a period of grief for the loss of Bellavista. After the State redistributed the mountain in minuscule plots of land, the government in power at the time took the leader of the peasant squatters to the podium of the United Nations to boast about the success of agrarian reform.

Polancho was the illegitimate son of don Nacianceno. Everyone in Bellavista knew who Polancho's father was except Nacianceno. His mother washed and ironed our clothing. She would bring Polancho by the hand, and would sit him on a kitchen bench. She liked spending the day at the hacienda because her son could eat like a pig. I would give him a tamal, and the boy would wolf it down with the voracity of a crocodile. He didn't even leave the banana leaves that wrapped the tamal on the plate. I never heard Polancho's voice, and he communicated with his mother through signs. She would tell me that her son was stupid. I didn't see him again until he was an adolescent and don Nacianceno asked me to let him harvest coffee. He stayed in Bellavista until the day that don Nacianceno, his mother and a little sister had their throats cut. The boy ran away and for years I knew nothing about him. However, on the day I saw his photo in the newspaper, standing next to the

Minister of Agriculture, I recognized his furtive look that had not changed since he was a child.

Polancho traveled to most countries in South America as a spokesman and an example of the Colombian government's new policies of land ownership. He didn't know how to read or write, but the government officials used his ignorance to lead to ruin those same peasants that he represented, and among them me. Bit by bit, Bellavista was unstitched, like a patchwork bedspread. The dispossessed had to sell their two hectares of land because they were dying of hunger. The government lent them money for the harvest, but they couldn't repay, and many had to mortgage their tiny plots of land. Naturally, the bank foreclosed on the land and auctioned it off cheaply. The squatters didn't foresee the harshness of the weather, the unending summers and ruining the coffee crop. Bellavista had been divided in an arbitrary manner: some lots had water but couldn't be planted because they were hollow and nothing grew in those godforsaken places; in other lots, one could sow two rows of coffee, but they did not receive even a drop of water. Some couldn't even transport a sack of coffee because there were no roads. Those who remained on the side of the road couldn't harvest a single tomato because when the river rose, it swept everything in its path.

The government had the best intentions with Bellavista and used its tyranny to convince an entire nation and a continent that it was possible to achieve progress. Other governments came, and Polancho was given more land to keep him quiet and forget about the insurrection in Bellavista. When Polancho wanted a bigger share from the Ministry of Agriculture, the Minister's private secretary told him that the office was not a public charity. Years later, Polancho told me in a letter, in which he asked for my help, that the authorities were looking for him because he was accused of being a bandit. It was true; the son of the washerwoman became one of the most sought after men in the country. A reward was offered for any information leading to Polancho, the fool. He was charged with stealing from the national treasury and for violating the security of the State. In a raid by more than a hundred soldiers and the police, he was peppered with bullets. He was trying to escape his lover's house on a farm near Barcelona.

Polancho had been portrayed by the national press as one of the most bloodthirsty assassins in the country's history. But no one remembered that he had started the takeover of Bellavista and that he was the product of a world as violent as himself that seemed to take a toll on everyone. Also, in 1976, I remember reading a special report in *El Tiempo* that Alfonso, my noble friend and lawyer, had also been shot by two apparently unknown men when he was leaving his office in Bogotá.

Chapter XIX

MY EXILE

During this period, I lost Fabio. I had baptized him with the same name as the twin who had died a few days after birth. They looked so alike that I imagined that God had given him back to me so that he could fulfill his late brother's destiny. I had sent him to Medellín to study law. I needed a legal representative in the family who would not steal from me and, even if he did so, it would be all in the family. Every time there were problems at the university, he came to Armenia and stayed while the protests continued.

Fabio's sudden death was always a mystery to me. From the moment of his sudden disappearance, I withdrew from everyone. In September 1965 Fabio had turned 26. He was a champion biker, played basketball and soccer. Every time he needed money he called me "my little treasure." I winked at him so that he could take money out of the drawer in my desk. He was like a continuation of the spirit of Octavio but in the body of Fabio, the little twin. He had the thick eyebrows and full lips of his father. I was worried that he would marry before he finished his studies because he had a lot of girlfriends. I had heard the rumors of his adventures. I didn't criticize until he went beyond the limits with Estelita Tarquino, the daughter of the godparents of one of my children, in the Berlín neighborhood. The girl had become a very handsome, graceful mulatto woman with a tiny waist. From her own mouth I heard words of dislike when she came to visit me and brought me some pastries. She was walking along 21st street in Armenia when she heard someone was honking at her from a truck. It was Fabio.

"Where can I take you, beautiful?" my son asked.

She got into the truck. He immediately put his open hand on the seat when she sat on the cushion.

"Idiot! What is wrong with you? Don't be fresh," she ranted. "Don't you see that I am like a sister?"

Estelita was right because the Tarquinos were like my own daughters. However, I had my doubts about this story, so I questioned Fabio in front of Estelita and he blushed.

"Mom, she was so gorgeous that I couldn't control myself."

Later, Fabio confessed that he hadn't recognized her on the street because he hadn't seen her since he left for boarding school and, later, the university. Nevertheless, the daughter of my neighbors in Berlín forgave him his fault, and at times I think she even provoked him. It was at the same Estela who saved him from being gored. She warned him that a runaway bull was at his back. It was a custom that the cattle being led to the slaughterhouse were driven along the streets, so it was necessary to close windows and doors along their way. If someone wanted to see the enraged cattle, they had to do so from the balconies or the roofs of their houses. That day, Fabio was going to go fishing with his friends in the Quindío River but the Willy jeeps got stuck in the middle of the muddy street. Everyone got to push without knowing that the animals were on the same street and getting close. Estelita saw them through the shutters of the window of her aunt's house, and barely had time to yell to Fabio that the beast was at his back. My son scaled the walkway, which was a meter higher than the street, and jumped, through a window that was half open. For a few seconds he felt that this was the end. He himself told me.

Sometimes he acted like his father because he was usually going from one mountain to another, but instead of traveling on horseback he rode his bicycle. He even rode with his team to Mérida, in Venezuela. He sent me postcards and packages with the medals he won in the towns. I understood little of sports, and he patiently explained how races and the interleague soccer championships were won. I personally took care of his uniforms and, though I didn't see any future in his running behind a ball, I unconditionally supported him.

I was frying some cheese the afternoon I was informed that my son was in the hospital. At first I thought, he had fallen off the bicycle and he is only hurt. He had been brought home several times on a stretcher with his knees skinned. But when I entered the emergency unit and saw the faces of his siblings, I knew it was something serious. He was bleeding from the aorta and the doctors couldn't stop the hemorrhage. Everyone in the family gave blood and his friends brought donors, even his distant relatives collaborated to save his life. Even though the blood wasn't compatible, another could use it. Felipe Jaramillo, a friend who was at the scene and was in the waiting room, told me that Fabio had been playing Russian roulette with Gustavo Osorio, another of his best friends, and the revolver went off. Fabio's girlfriend told another version and broke into tears.

"Fabio and Gustavo exchanged guns but Gustavo knew that his was loaded," she said hysterically.

The police inspector told me that a Communist had shot at him from a balcony. The son of the owner of the house where they got together to play cards, and where the crime took place, didn't see anything because he was in the bathroom. Some neighbors who heard the shot saw a young man in a checked shirt jump through a window. Doña Azucena, who sold gladiolas in the market for people to take to the cemetery, once told me it was Conservative conspiracy.

Gustavo, my son's supposed friend, escaped from Armenia by a bus that belonged to the Palmira fleet. I never heard his version of the events. The truth was that my son was dead and nothing could revive him. Everything was so confusing and absurd that I found it impossible to believe what had happened. I had given a gun to Fabio for his own protection, but not for him to commit suicide.

The expropriation of Bellavista had been one of the hardest blows I had received in life, but the death of another son was unsurpassable. It was like a hammer blow that left me without the strength to fight. I didn't eat or sleep, and I started to hate humanity. I felt powerless and without the strength to ask something of God because I could not look Him in the face. I lost my faith. More than that, I lost my self-confidence. In what had I failed as a mother if all I had worked for was for my children? Where was my mistake? How could I help the three children I still had?

I was ashamed of myself because I thought I didn't deserve to live, but I didn't deny the possibility of starting to rebuild the pieces of life I still had. At this stage, I didn't think a man would rescue me or that God would take me out of the hole I was in. On the contrary, I was the one who had to bring about my own salvation.

When I opened my eyes, after sleeping an hour between five and six in the morning, I felt as if the world was crushing me. I continued managing the properties, fighting with the lawyers, answering letters and paying debts to the banks. However, I could not concentrate. I wasn't even happy while drinking white kennel corn milk with cornmeal cakes. I couldn't deal with my bad mood. My blonde hair was thinning and dull. What little I had left was turning grey.

When I was young I paid no attention to my appearance even though Rosario would tell me to smarten up and to use a lot of perfume when Jesús came home. The only thing I had that resembled perfume was a bottle of agua florida de Murray cologne. I would sprinkle it on my arms and face to refresh myself. Now I had spots on my face. From my neck, arms and stomach my skin hung, full of fat. I noticed that my body was wearing out and I could not hide the varicose veins that I had in both legs. I learned to use opaque stockings to hide the mess of nerves that descended my extremities. They entered my feet, as if they were looking for an exit so they could dig themselves into the ground. Doctor Orozco said that there was nothing to do to cure them except try to avoid the rupture of a vein. On the other hand, I felt my petrified bones inside me and, though I wanted to escape from that iron armour, other forces pulled at me from head to toe. My left hand, which was fractured when I fell off a horse when I was escaping from some robbers, knit after years, but never regained its natural mobility. It was like a claw that served only to pick up certain light things. I put on the first thing I found in the closet, and for a long period of time I didn't notice that I always wore the same black velvet dress. I didn't even powder my face, the only makeup I had ever used in my life.

In a way, I had opted to stay by myself in a mansion that I had bought on Avenida Bolívar in Armenia. My three children had gone off to live in foreign parts and there was no chance of returning to the rural areas. Armenia continued to be a provincial city where everyone knew everyone. The main avenue made its way toward the north, and the streetlights and sewers only reached the Bavaria brewery, located near the end of town. I had Neftalí, a driver who took me everywhere.

Diagonally across from my residence, the city's bishop lived in a glass mansion. He lived there with two nuns and a green apple tree in the central garden of the patio. For many months, which then became years, I never entered a chapel. Most of the priests I knew had children and others had retired from the priesthood to marry their concubines. Those who, from the pulpit, had pointed us out to the Liberals and called us a menace to the divine order had gotten more money than a priest with three parishes. In the same way, I had lost my faith in the saints and if I got close to the bishop it was because he let me use his private library. I was one of the few who were allowed access to the mansion and his prayer rooms. The Monsignor slept in a bed so high that he needed a ladder to climb into it. Well, he was also short and his habit made him appear to be stuck to the floor. He was younger than I and from his features it seemed that he had been good looking when he was studying in the Manizales seminary. At first, and because of protocol, each time I visited him I kissed his ring but after a while he said that so much reverence wasn't necessary. He would send the nuns over to my house with apples and I returned the basket full of some fried cheese as big as grapefruits. He asked me what my secret was to make them so big and unbroken because the nuns had tried to repeat my formula with no success. The secret was to add a little bit of bicarbonate of soda, sprinkle them with brown sugar water and fry them in very hot oil. The Monsignor complained about the food prepared by the nuns and said that the poor women could not differentiate between salt and sugar. They added salt to the coffee with milk and on holy days they cooked fish with sugar.

The Monsignor's bedroom was connected to another bedroom that had an altar. To the right, a hallway connected his room to the library. His religious books were flanked by those of philosophy, the *Cántico espiritual* of San Juan de la Cruz and the documents of the Second Vatican Council. From Rome he brought me a certificate with my name and sealed by John XXIII. He also gave me a Murano scapular amulet. I carried it in my handbag like an amulet.

I plunged into reading *Anna Karenina*, *The Brothers Karamazov*, *Oliver Twist*, *War and Peace*, *Red and Black* and a novel titled *Limelight*. The Monsignor had a world map and with his finger he showed me the location of Russia, England, France and Spain. He knew all the great figures of the books and admired Peter the Great, Catherine the Great and Napoleon. I once heard him say he had visited Napoleon's tomb in Paris. I preferred the figure of the strategist who had reached the gates of Moscow. We spent long hours chatting about the biographies of Thomas Jefferson, George Washington and other names that I do not remember. My life was nothing like theirs and I couldn't see any difference between a character in a novel and the history of these men. Anything could happen on paper, and I had come to have heated discussions with Monsignor because I told him that the lives of these heroes were very simple. On one other occasion, Monsignor could not convince me that man had reached the moon. In the Vatican library he had seen a piece of a moon rock, which was presented by the gringo government to the Pope. I wouldn't believe the story of the moon just because I had seen it on the television or because Monsignor confirmed it.

My mistrust of Monsignor's words grew the more I read novels or biographies. The contents of those books had nothing to do with my reality. My monologues made Monsignor laugh and, as a reflex, I began to notice that he was laughing at me. Without knowing it, Monsignor had become a sort of filter for my ignorance and he had made my doubts grow.

Our friendship continued by mail because he was sent to Medellín to teach theology. When he left, he gave me part of his book collection.

PART IV

DIONISIO

❊ ❊ ❊

D ionisio quit his career as a priest, and he went to Buenos Aires to study music. At first I often received his correspondence: Dear Mom: The streets and the buildings of this port city look like those of Paris, Madrid, Rome or London...". I had never heard of the City of Lights but I had seen ink drawings made by Monsignor. The city had the Nueve de Julio Avenue, a street with eight lanes wider than Bolívar Avenue in Armenia or Jiménez in Bogotá, which was filled with many cars. Dionisio told me that the Colón Theater was a Creole copy of the Scala of Milan. In front of the train station was a replica of Big Ben. In the spring, the parks smelled of *jacarandas, lapachas* and *palo de borracho* trees. The Plaza de Mayo was filled with *cauchos, tipas* and palms, like I once saw in Buga when I went to fulfill a promise I had made to Our Lord of miracles. I think I hadn't been aware before of the aroma of the city, but Dionisio made me realize that Armenia was infused with the fragrance of roasted coffee except for Bolivar Plaza, which every night was perfumed by jasmine. The sweet odor of the *veraneras* and the *sanjoaquines* flowers that adorned the sidewalks of the avenue blended with the aroma of the fried orange waffles, the peanuts, the mangoes with salt and the coconuts sold by the street vendors.

On Florida Street he bought a box of *alfajores* sweets that he sent with someone traveling to our area. I know because on the bottom of the box I found the address: Alfajores La Avellaneda, Florida number 9 (1009). Buenos Aires, Republic of Argentina. I had never tried these sweets and I loved the filling of *arequipe,* caramel or *dulce de leche*, as the Argentines called it.

The women wore fur coats during the winter and in summer, when vacationing on the beaches of Mar del Plata, they used sport clothes. Some wore hats with feathers and others were wide brimmed ones. In the photographs he sent, my son looked incredibly handsome in the middle of all those long-faced girls of very white countenances. In one of my letters I asked him if everyone in Argentina danced the tango. He told me sincerely that, till then, no one he knew listened to or knew how to dance the tango. Dionisio assured me that the girls that he went out with thought Carlos Gardel was the name of a candy store on Humboldt Street. I could see Jesús and his tender eyes on the day he was told that Gardel had died in a plane crash in Medellín. I had never seen him so sad except when Rosario got married and left with her husband. I think I hated the tango because it reminded me of Jesús' adventures and absences. The old man was depressed for a while but I know it was easier for him to remember the lyrics of *Mi Buenos Aires querido* or *Cuesta abajo* than the names of his own children.

Dionisio told me that the sound of the "l" and the "y" where not like ours and that's why at first he didn't understand many words. As the years passed, Dionisio acquired Argentine expressions and customs. Instead of eating cornmeal cakes with sausage he ate Spanish tortilla accompanied by a baguette. He called a guava dessert a *membrillo* and, if it was accompanied by cheese, it was a *bocado de vigilante,* a watch man's snack, as those who lived in Boca, an Italian neighborhood, called it. It was so named because it was the supper of the night guards. The *sudado* that I prepared with potatoes, yucca, brisket and sometime ripe plantain, Dionisio called *puchero.* It was all the same to me as long as he ate what I prepared for him. No one had drunk wine in my house or lit a cigarette or anything like it since Jesús had died. But Dionisio arrived with a pipe in his mouth and even the basement of the house was saturated with a smell of marigold flowers.

In Armenia's cafés, near the market, he drank coffee with cheese bread, fried cheese or beef patties but he began to call them *confitería.* I once asked him what that word meant because I associated it with confetti or caramels. He told me it was like a small bar where people drank espresso and ate ice cream or French style pastries. I told him to cut it out because we weren't in France and we weren't on the Mayo Avenue either. I was very frank and I told him not to confuse a *tamal* with an *alfajor* or a ginger cookie with a *medialuna,* some kind of croissant. The closest thing to a confitería was El Destapado, a place where people drank coffee and conducted businesses. I was one of the few women who entered because it was a place reserved for men. The only other women in El Destapado were the lottery and cigarette vendors. The coffee growers, cattlemen and sales agents got used to my presence and treated me with great respect. I also became very angry when he changed the names of the *chunchurria,* the livers, the gizzards and the heart to *picada,* Argentine barbecue. After all, entrails were the same everywhere.

Dionisio stayed in Coronel Pringles, a hotel that belonged to some of Mister Bremer's relatives. Each month I sent him enough dollars to cover the rent, his meals and his studies at the Conservatory. He had arrived in Buenos Aires during a very hard winter and I had to send him more money to buy coats, mufflers, gloves and boots. Mister Bremer hadn't recognized him when he went to pick him up at the airport. He had grown a moustache and was starting to go prematurely bald. Mister Bremer was almost blind and he dictated letters to his niece in which he told me about my son. Mister Bremer compared Juan Domingo Perón to Adolph Hitler and my son proudly told me that his classmates went to the marches that supported Perón the dictator. His college classmates were the children of high government officials.

I had reached these mountains riding on a mule, with one change of clothing and no money. I had seen Armenia grow around the market and calle 18. In a few decades it had become a provincial town filled with bars, a few brothels, four schools, three coffee warehouses, two parks, a cathedral, the municipal post office, city hall, and the Bolivar Theater. On the contrary, my son had arrived in a metropolis on a plane. He didn't have to look for a job because he was going to study. On many occasions I asked myself if, by leaving me and the life he so detested, he wasn't also running away from himself. Dionisio didn't go to the soda fountain or accompany his brothers to the Sunday afternoon soccer matches. Bullfights made him nauseous, and he had no idea of what to talk about to girls his age because according to him, they were very silly. I also noticed that he didn't get along with the other boys either. I wasn't surprised that he didn't hang out on a corner with his classmates from the San José school, leaning against the wall and ogling the girls that left the Capuchine or the Official schools in the afternoons. Dionisio spent hours in the living room of the house with his ear glued to the radio listening to the soap operas or repeating the Casta Diva aria from Norma opera sung by Maria Callas on the gramophone.

The monuments of Buenos Aires and Evita Peron's deeds did not dazzle me. For my son, the city would be his best discovery because it would start to conquer his soul. He would not have to hunt or cut down trees, as his father and I had done, but he would have to come to terms with himself in a new territory. I arrived there when there weren't even roads; my son arrived in a place where he could stroll along the boulevards to the movies or the ports.

I had stopped receiving any more signs of life from Mister Bremer. Then, through Dionisio, I heard that he died of a heart attack. Months before, Dionisio had left the hotel of the relatives of the now deceased Mister Bremer. He lived in an apartment on San Telmo with a Peruvian student whose last name was Matto. In his letters, he didn't tell me anymore about his singing classes or the piano he wanted to buy. Now he told me about Evita's speeches. He treated her like she was his girlfriend. He had memorized the words she said on the radio, and he sent them to me written like musical notes on paper. He knew the itinerary of her visits to the poor neighborhoods and hospitals of Buenos Aires, and had a scrapbook about her filled with newspaper clippings. He once sent me one where Evita appeared greeting the Pope. In truth, she was very beautiful, just like he described her. According to the newspapers, her jewelry was very expensive and Chanel designed custom made suits for her in Paris.

Dionisio didn't write to me for a period of five months, and I thought he was in the hospital or something similar. Through the Colombian consulate in Buenos Aires, I was able to locate him. He hadn't wanted to even talk with his friends since the death of Evita Perón. On the day of her funeral, he borrowed a uniform from the son of an admiral and disguised himself as one of the guards who kept watch over Evita Perón's casket. No one discovered him and he was able to see her up close.

When I read that General Perón had been overthrown, I sent Dionisio a ticket home. However, he responded in a telegram and told me that all was well and no one bothered him because he was a foreign student. I had to keep sending him more and more money because it was never enough. Now he told me that he was perfecting his voice with a singing professor called Abel Piazza, who had been a student of Enrico Caruso. Dionisio felt honored to be in his class because Maestro Piazza chose his own students. His expenses, among them the professor's fees, had gone up. According to my son, the maestro had his studio on a third floor on Lavalle Street and he was connected with radio people. The professor had told him that he could make his debut during one of the Sunday programs.

Years later, standing at the foot of my bed, he confessed and asked for my forgiveness because the funds I had sent him for the piano were given to the Peruvian because he owed him money, but everything that had to do with Professor Piazza was true. After the occasional class however, he went to the theater and stayed till dawn watching vaudeville or Libertad Lamarque movies. Dionisio wasn't going to the Conservatory anymore or to private classes with the tenor. There were frequent parties in the San Telmo apartment until the owner threw them out, due to the noise. When mail had been returned to me, I thought it was a mistake.

I began to have doubts about my son's academic advances when he wrote asking me to send more money because he thought a singer had more of a future in Milan than in Armenia. His new project was to go to Europe with my money. Many of his Buenos Aires friends had gone to Paris because they thought their city was boring, the people spoke only about soccer and, even worse, there was no culture. The reasons his acquaintances, poets, writers, actors or composers gave for leaving the city didn't convince me. I had been an immigrant, but I hadn't gone to the ends of the earth to get what I wanted. Armenia wasn't really the center of the universe. In all its nooks and crannies and during all its eras, poems had been written even though good poetry was scarce in those days. He would have to return to his country, to his province and his home to prove that even a morsel of blood sausage merited a few sonnets.

I immediately sent him the return ticket. In a note I told him that if he did not come back, I would cut him out of my will. In a month he returned with ten suitcases and a Japanese folding fan in his hand. In his heart he was sure that I wasn't up to fulfilling my threat of leaving him out of my will, but he wasn't willing to risk it. Besides, when he found out that there was no cash in the bank, he packed his books, his bowties, and the photo of Evita Perón and returned.

I knew my children very well. When it had to do with money, they couldn't hide their ambition. Dionisio claimed his part of his father's inheritance. He was of age and believed that he had a claim to his father's estate. He was a widower, though he had never told me that he had married a woman from Buenos Aires. I found out when I found a visa application form for France among his papers. On it was his name and that of his wife: Dionisio Márquez González; marital status: married; wife: Victoria Musali de Márquez. In his letters he never told me about his marriage, and much less about the death of my daughter-in-law. Victoria had died of leukemia after a year of marriage. I knew her through a photo he showed me. She was a very beautiful woman with abundant black hair. If it weren't for her sad look, I would say she looked like me. Matto, his Peruvian friend, introduced them in the music faculty, and three months later they were secretly married. She continued to live with her parents. The two kids participated in the Peronista youth groups, and helped the committees in charge of distributing food in the poor neighborhoods of Buenos Aires. Victoria's illness cut her time short, and Dionisio visited her tomb in the Recoleta every day while he was in the city.

Very soon I understood that, more than the sum of money he claimed, he was urgently asking for his freedom. He had always had everything in his life, and it was time for him to realize that the stars were not fried cheese and the moon was not fried cheese, either. It wasn't easy for me to cut the strings and, much less, to deny him a cent if he spent his father's inheritance carousing. It bothered me to reveal my vulnerability. So I sold off some of my stocks, and some of my properties to cover his share, and opened a bank account in his name, but without his knowledge, so that there could be some reserves. Since Jesús had died, I had been the administrator of all our properties, and I knew that, sooner or later, our children would ask for the account balances.

He left his suitcases and the photo of Evita in the house on Bolivar Avenue, and went to Mexico with the money. In his letters he told me he took acting classes in the Universidad Autónoma de México. He was signed up for the third course, called Berthold Brecht. I was glad he was happy, but being an actor in the mountains was like planting an orchid in a pigsty. Actors died of hunger or joined a circus.

I was tormented by the idea that he might not marry again or settle down, even if it was in Patagonia. I became calmer when he later wrote to me and told me that he had noticed that his true vocation was to be a composer. My musical knowledge was very limited and it never dawned on me that a composer was like a writer. Composers told stories or expressed their frustrations through their songs and, besides, they earned more money than an actor. But I remembered a biography of Mozart lent to me by Monsignor, and I would get goose bumps thinking that my son would end up in a pauper's grave. I didn't doubt his talent, but I did doubt his capacity to control his spoiled child like impulses.

From Mexico he sent me records of 78 revolutions. I bought a Motorola record player that looked like a cupboard. Marta María, my youngest daughter, would put on the music and I spent hours listening to my son's songs. I was proud of him and his work. The lyrics of the songs were love stories that ended tragically, songs of admiration about mothers or odes to the coffee plantations. Sometimes the maids called me into the kitchen, because they were listening to Lucho Gatica, Leo Marini or Toña la Negra singing some of his songs on the radio. His new loves were María Felix, Javier Solís, Pedro Infante and Antonio Aguilar, whom he had met in person. He even had a photo of María Felix by his side.

Dionisio stayed in Mexico for ten years. When he left Aztec lands to return to Colombia, he arrived with twenty trunks and a dozen friends. Upon his return from Argentina he had only brought half the amount of luggage. He had a beard and his head was bald. He appeared older than his years, and he looked very handsome in his white suit and wine colored silk bow tie. He bought me three mantillas, a bag full of jalapeño peppers because I liked chilies, an image of the Virgin of Guadalupe and a pencil drawing of my face when I was young. He also gave me a small parrot that sang Happy Birthday, the *Ave María* and some of his songs. The bird died a few weeks after arriving in Armenia because Dionisio had fed him wine in Mexico, and I gave him bread with chocolate. He also brought a retinue of singers and Don Leo Marini, whose appearance didn't match his voice. He showed up at my door. He was small, had a little black moustache and put on too much hair gel. He dressed in pastel colored suits, and was very sweet. He drank wine with breakfast, lunch and supper. I think that when he went to the theater to perform, he was already tipsy.

My house became a five star hotel. By the time I finally noticed, I had become the servant of Dionisio's guests. The kitchen was always open, there were never enough sheets to change the beds every day, and the maids complained about the odor of the cigarettes smoked by the artists. I reached my breaking point with their mariachis. You couldn't even use the bathrooms because there was always some star performer in them. One day I found a guitar on my bed and I told Dionisio to look for his own home in which to attend to his business. My tolerance had its limits.

The musicians never returned to my home on Bolívar Avenue in Armenia or to Colombia. There was no free hotel and Dionisio lost a lot of money as a show business agent. So he opened a record shop to sell his own recordings but sales were so low that he couldn't even pay the rent. He opened a night club, but early on had to close it for lack for clients. Dionisio told me it was just a matter of time, until people found out about the place. But I knew they wouldn't go to Los Diamantes, as the bar was called, because no one wanted to listen to mediocre singers with strange names like Marlowe. But he said that this was how great talents, like Javier Solís and Cantinflas, had been discovered.

On the contrary, the public only wanted to dance cumbias and make love in the shadowy corners of the dark bar. How they hated it when, microphone in hand, he betrayed his nighttime visitors:

—A special greeting to Doctor Arango, who is at table number three —Dionisio would say, thinking he was doing them a favor. Except this was how he scared people away because the bosses didn't want their wives to know of their affairs with their secretaries. My son was convinced that everything would work in the manner of the nightclubs in Mexico. He was naïve because a dive in the basement of a provincial city was not the right place in which to recite poems. Dionisio failed to understand that here you cried silently when you heard the lyrics of tangos and milongas, where a night club was a monument to entertainment and not a place to spill your guts.

Dionisio told me to my face that he was a miscarriage of nature. I reproached him his treachery because he was standing in front of one who had suffered. At 42 years of age, he felt like an outsider. When I observed him, I felt ashamed and at the same time angry that he had done nothing with his life and that he also blamed others for his errors. It was very easy for him to transfer his faults to others and it was demoralizing to see that I couldn't help him fight his own battles. I had fought my own and my only comfort was my work. I had not given into my weaknesses, and fought like a lioness to protect my cubs. I had had no time to think about how sad I was because, if I had, I wouldn't be telling this story. How was it that a being I had created couldn't face his own conflicts? Where were my genes and those of his father? But at this point in my life, I didn't feel so guilty because Dionisio had had more than he ever could have expected.

It took me a lifetime to accept Dionisio with all his faults, his failures, and his arrogance. I think that only at the end of my existence I finally understood that I had made him not out of strong oak, but that he was as vulnerable as the little egg of a Cuban chicken. As time passed, his resentment towards me grew just as did his disillusionment with himself did. In everyday acts I felt the stab of his words. I took care of his meals and he responded placing the plate on the floor. He said that what I prepared was dog food. The mongrels that I had at the farms showed infinite gratitude with their tails, which banged against my skirt when I gave them leftovers. My own son looked at me with resentment when I prepared his steaks almost raw, the way he liked them. He wouldn't say a word to me for weeks, and then he would show up in my bedroom with a bouquet of flowers.

Chapter XXI

MY DAUGHTER

Marta María was my only daughter, and she was not an exception to obligatory exile. Like her brothers, she also had to leave the mountains for fear of kidnapping or something worse. The nuns of La Presentación in Medellín were in charge or her education. I had neither the time nor the patience to dedicate myself to my daughter. The nuns convinced me that they would do a good job, and I delegated the responsibility of forming Marta María's character to them. Her faced looked like mine, but she didn't have my character. I knew it from the moment she was born; in the precise instant the wet nurses took charge of her, because she was born premature at 7 months. Fabio, my other son, and Marta were born a year apart and made their first communion together. They were good friends, and Fabio protected her from her older brothers.

The nuns sent me good reports of her behavior and her grades. I almost never saw her because I didn't leave the farms, and she was out of my reach. When she turned fifteen, I gave her a gold brooch shaped like the sun. I remember that I threw a party on the terrace surrounding the pool of the house on Bolivar Avenue and I had a dress of tulle made for her. The skirt stood out and was shot through with celestial colors. My daughter had pretty legs and her breasts were big, like mine when I was young. Girls her age combed their hair like in the photos I had seen of Evita Perón. I didn't allow her to use lipstick or to paint a beauty mark near her lips. Neither her brothers nor I let any boys come near the house. I didn't want her to marry yet because she was still a child. I wanted her to enjoy her youth and beauty. In fact, when I found out she was receiving secret notes from a suitor; I made arrangements with the nuns of La Presentación for her to go to Washington to study English.

Marta María stayed in the United States for a few years, but she didn't learn the language. It was the spring of 1959 in Washington. In the photos that she sent me by mail, she appeared with her friend María Teresa, from Bucaramanga, near the Potomac River. Their black uniforms and berets contrasted with the flowers of the Japanese cherry blossoms. The trees scattered their flowers on the lawns even though the monuments were meticulously clean. I never visited the capital of the United States, but I was content with the knowledge that she was walking on the ground of the best country in the world.

I wanted her to stay there and marry a gringo or at least someone of her social class, but she didn't pay any attention to María Teresa's brother, Esteban, who adored her. The boy was studying engineering at Harvard, and visited his sister frequently in the boarding school run by the sisters of La Presentación. This was how he met Marta María. He accompanied them on their Sunday strolls around the White House.

Marta María had kept all of Esteban's love letters, even after she married another man. This is why I was able to read the correspondence that I found with the photos. Esteban and María Teresa were children of a magnate from Santander. Their father, afraid of a kidnapping, sent him out of the country first. Then he arranged everything for María Teresa's departure from the country. My daughter told me that her friend was very elegant, but stole candies from Woolworth's, a store similar to our Ley shops. Marta María told me that her friend confessed she had a disease called kleptomania. The poor girl couldn't control her itch to steal something every time an opportunity presented itself. I told my daughter not to go out with her, because if the police caught her and she was with María Teresa they would both go to jail, even though she had nothing to do with the whole thing. My daughter promised she wouldn't see her anymore but her will was so weak that her friend swayed her and told her she'd try to control her hands.

I was very happy that Esteban was courting Marta María, maybe this way she would forget her boyfriend in Colombia. But I have always believed that chickens left the corn strewn in the patio to end up eating shit on the coffee plantation. My daughter encouraged Esteban and even when she returned to the country, he phoned her regularly. When he found out that she was married, he shot himself in the head in the university dorm. My daughter was so conceited and inconsiderate that she never had the guts to tell the boy the truth about her feelings.

From Washington, and without my permission, she continued to correspond with a nobody and when she returned, she married him in secret. Her never do well husband didn't like to work, but did like having women to support him. I didn't need detectives for news of his escapades to reach my ears, because even the vegetable sellers in the market were aware of them. He had two mistresses, both older than him, and sterile. Later on I found out that he had no paternal feelings and he felt no shame in admitting that he didn't like children. However, his lovers accepted him as he was and stayed with him.

He pawned all the jewels I gave to my daughter, even the pin shaped like a sun that I gave her when she turned fifteen. When I demanded the pin back, Marta María said that thieves had broken into the house and had taken her jewelry box. He was thrown out of all the places in which I found work for him. I gave him the management of El Vergel, one of my haciendas, and he gave me no reports of the sales of coffee or bananas. According to him, the hacienda only produced losses and with the coffee harvest he paid the debts.

His father was the owner of a car parts store, and he had a young mistress with six children as well as the three legitimate ones he had with his wife. Rosita, my daughter's mother in law, even knew where her rival lived and the names of all the children, but didn't have the guts to leave him because he never failed to provide food or pay the rent. Rosita's face never showed a slightest sign of anger or frustration. Every morning she went to six o'clock mass and came back with a smile, as if things would change because she prayed to San Antonio to return her husband to her. I didn't sit in judgment of her for ignoring that her husband was cheating on her because Jesús hadn't been Saint Francis of Assisi precisely. I had caught my husband giving the maids money by hiding it among the socks. I admired Rosita's devotion, her faith and naiveté. On the other hand, I didn't think that God would work without my help, and if I prayed in my hours of anger it was because I begged Him to get my husband off my back. For God's sake, may God protect me, but I am telling the truth.

Rosita told me that 'out of sight, out of mind' but I had my eyes in my head, not in my heart. Among women of my generation, infidelity was accepted as a part of daily life and, as long as the men met their paternal obligations, the issue about lovers was not brought up. After all, they were women of the streets. But what happened in the case that the other became number one? Until the day she died, Rosita continued to believe that don Pablo, her husband, respected and loved her more than the other.

Don Pablo, my daughter's father in law, was a tightwad and wouldn't give my grandchildren even a candy but, with all the children he had to feed, I couldn't blame him. My son-in-law was handsome, and I was displeased that my daughter was so shallow that she had fallen in love with him because of his appearance. When he was 12, he was already drinking *aguardiente* liquor at the local cantinas with his schoolmates from the Rufino School and, as an adult, his attraction to drink and marijuana grew. Neither Don Pablo nor Rosita smoked. For the first time in my life I heard the word marijuana and, at first, I thought it was marjoram, used to flavor chicken soup. My eldest son explained what it was and how kids used it. There is nothing hidden in God's vineyard. I learned that my son-in-law was a pothead because the farm hands found him smoking. My son-in-law drugged himself under my nose and I thought he was a fool.

Doña Berta, a neighbor who had known him since he was a child, was puzzled and asked me how it was possible that my daughter had set her sights on such a man when there were so many others in the world. I had asked myself the same thing many times. I always concluded that it was partly my responsibility because of the strict education I had given her.

I think what made me the angriest was when she came home with black eyes. How could my daughter allow that son of a bitch to hit her? Jesús had tried it once with me, but he regretted it because I broke a piece of firewood on his back and Doctor Fajardo had to bind him up for a month. But the worst part was that Marta María didn't leave him. She was afraid of him, and returned to the feet of her master so that he could kick her. I couldn't fathom that my daughter was spineless and, even worse, had no self-esteem. I finally understood that she had no willpower to leave him, but I did have the power to stop the destruction of my daughter by a psychopath. Thanks to my son-in-law, Marta María had lost her first baby when she was five months pregnant because he kicked her in the stomach. My daughter had lied to me and said that she had fallen from a bus. Later on I found out that her husband had beaten her because the neighbors that lived on the first floor heard the blows. They lived in a house with a balcony in a modest neighborhood and I paid the rent. They didn't have a telephone but the tenant who lived on the first floor had a store from which he called me to tell me about my son-in-law's coming and goings. I tipped don José for his services and once he had to call the police because he thought Marta had committed suicide. Marta had thrown herself from the window carrying her eldest son because her husband was beating her. It was a miracle that nothing happened to her when she fell onto don José's patio. When I reached her, because don José called me, Marta was on the floor crying and hugging her son. The wretch had escaped through the balcony.

I brought her and my grandchildren home, even though my other children and friends objected. Even her bothers tried to stop her from entering the house. Leonardo said that she was a married woman and her husband had to support her. But I couldn't throw my daughter—who had three children—out to the street, even though her husband had no shame. I forced her to divorce him because I couldn't afford to keep supporting her along with any additional babies. With the help of my lawyers I was able, in a few months, to separate their assets, but not obtain the annulment of Marta María's Catholic marriage. When I picked her up with her furniture, she was very thin and answered in monosyllables. I had to take care of my grandchildren because she had become withdrawn. Marta María spent the nights awake, and it took a few years for her to recover her tranquility. I took her to several specialists, and I even got her the cross of Caravaca because I was told that it scared away bad spirits. In her exhausting hours of insomnia she would hear a chained dog creep around her bed. Her hallucinations made me ill, but the medicines and the garlic that I gave her helped her overcome the crisis.

Chapter XXII

THE KIDNAPPING

My blood froze when Monsignor called me at midnight to confirm my suspicions. That morning Leonardo had not brought me milk or oranges from the farm. I thought he had stayed to sleep with one of his mistresses because his wife called me to complain that he hadn't gone home the night before. I immediately took a taxi and went to the house of *La Repolla*, one of his most fervent lovers. Rocío, known as *La Repolla* thanks to her legendary rear, came to the door in her nightgown and was not surprised to see me. She knew that someday I would show up to look for him. I had never gotten involved with my son's affairs but, when it came to his protection, I would do anything. We both surveyed each other from head to toe and then knew we were fighting for the same cause. She didn't know where Leonardo was either. Very early in the morning two days ago she had said goodbye to him with a hug and a kiss. She told me that that morning she had cried a lot and thought it had to do her guilty feelings and how sorry she felt for Leonardo's wife. Rocío reminded Leo of his responsibilities as a husband and every night told him that it was not a good idea to leave his young bride alone.

My son had good taste in women and *La Repolla* was no exception. Rocío was brown skinned and had a wide, firm backside. Her hair was short light brown, her eyes were very dark and the shape of her nose and mouth showed some evidence of white ancestry. My second son was already married, but he was always involved with other women. He had two illegitimate children and was very responsible about supporting them. The kids were not his with La Repolla but rather the product of his first love affair. Leonardo never wanted to give them his last name but always sent food and clothing. I don't know how many women he had because he was always very reserved; What I knew I found out thanks to the gossip that the cooks, the butlers and the drivers told me.

So what I was most afraid of came to pass. According to the administrator of the hacienda, my son didn't show up at the usual hour. The farmers found his truck without gasoline and registration documents. An agronomist and the driver who were traveling with him told the police and me everything that happened: It was approximately six in the morning and they were driving along, talking about the plans to uproot old coffee plants and plant Caturra, a new type of coffee. The National Federation of Coffee Growers recommended Caturra as the best option because, among other reasons, more plants could be planted in fewer hectares. It was said that its aroma and flavor were better than the others. I actually had more confidence in Bourbon and Arabica coffee than in the hybrids of the Federation. I myself had cultivated them all my life and, with good shade from guamo trees and rain, I brought in my harvests. But my son wanted to modernize the haciendas and bring in Brazilian machinery.

But let us return to the story. All of a sudden, and when they reached the Calamar Bridge, a red jeep cut them off and the driver had to stop. Four men, dressed in military uniforms and carrying machine-guns, jumped out of the vehicle. They told Leonardo that this was a kidnapping and that he should please accompany them. The agronomist and driver were tied up and abandoned by the side of the highway. They blindfolded and handcuffed Leo and took him away. According to the two witnesses, my son didn't stop resisting all the time. Leo kicked one of the kidnappers in the balls and yelled that they were all major sons of bitches. One of them didn't hesitate and knocked out his teeth with the butt of his gun.

From the first moment I knew the police would not be my best allies since, among other things, they didn't have that many resources. Because of this, Monsignor recommended I get in touch with Payares Peinado, an army general who received me that same night in his house. He gave me a shot of clear brandy liquor and I took a drink for the first and last time in my life. General Payares asked me many questions that I don't recall well now but there was one that left me thinking about the possibility that I had enemies. Who were these shameless people who hid their faces? Why had they chosen one of my sons? With what right did they deprive him of his liberty? I had no doubt that my son had things to account for but, as for what referred to me, I owed no money and had never harmed anyone. The only thing I had done in my life was work like a mule to have money to pay taxes and cover up my children's foolishnesses.

Payares Peinado came to my house the next day and gave me instructions: I was the only one who should answer the phone in a private room and could not tell my friends any details of my conversations with him. No one could know about our frequent meetings. Anyone that came to the house had to make an appointment, and I couldn't open the door if I did not know the visitor. All the house servants and the people working in the haciendas were suspect. For several months I couldn't even go to the corner without being watched. My employees' salaries were paid from an office in Armenia to avoid risks of any type. Payares had prepared me for the worst from the moment I contacted him.

After an anxious week, I received a letter that was shoved under the door and in which I was told that I should expect a phone call. Indeed, the kidnappers got in touch with me. Each time they called the house, I heard different voices, sometimes a woman, other times a man, and once they even used a child. The messages were cut off and they would hang up without letting me answer. I reported all the details to Payares and he wasn't surprised. It seemed he knew the habits of kidnappers very well and always anticipated the next move of the villains. His thick brows, which hid the color of his eyes, bothered me but I had to control myself and not cry in front of this stranger. General Payares was the only one who could do something for my son. However, I felt that military men and fortune-tellers were a bad omen. Since the death of my husband I had not visited the fortune tellers since I was afraid of knowing the future. But I had heard the song of the striped cuckoo bird in the garden, even before the disappearance of my son. It was not a good sign. I remember that a few days before Jesús's death, the bird didn't stop bothering everyone in the house in the Berlin neighborhood. To further aggravate my paranoia, a black butterfly the size of a turtledove clung to the wall of the bedroom my son used when he was single. The insect appeared there three days before the kidnapping. Even though I tried to scare it away, it didn't move. After two months of having no news about Leo, except for the calls, I decided to hire a woman who cast magic spells. Who cared, I had nothing to lose! The woman told me he was being held close by, in a dark room, and that he was very thin. Payares was furious when I told him what the fortune-teller had said.

"Señora, have faith but don't be fooled by swindlers. This is a matter of military intelligence," he repeated.

The constant ringing of the phone was driving me crazy, but Payares asked me to be patient because I was the connection to the kidnappers. They finally told me that if I wanted to see my son alive, I had to give them one hundred million pesos. Also they warned me not to speak to the DOS (Department of Security) or the military because, if I did, they would send me my son's body.

I told them I wanted to hear Leonardo's voice and they put him on the phone.

"I'm okay, Mom, and pay them what they're asking for."

It was as if someone else was talking with my son's voice. His tone was calm and didn't show any hostility. In fact, in the few words I exchanged with him during his kidnapping, I noticed an inexplicable sympathy towards his kidnappers.

Were they crazy? I didn't have that amount in cash and with the profit from the previous coffee harvest I had paid the loans from the *Caja Agraria* and the *Banco Cafetero*. I told them I didn't have that amount, and they told me it wasn't their problem, that I should borrow money from my rich friends. Payares Peinado was insufferable and told me to try to negotiate with them while he continued with the necessary investigations. The General said that the kidnappers would give themselves away sooner or later because, the more time went by, the chances of capturing them increased.

"Señora, they are common delinquents. They are not Communists," Payares Peinado said as he was drinking coffee.

Of course, it wasn't his son that was in this mess! I didn't care if his kidnappers were Conservatives, Liberals, bandits, Communists, guerrillas or plain old bad guys. In a moment of desperation, I told them that I had only gathered 50 million because everything else was invested. They told me that they would think about it and gave me their answer with an envelope that contained my son's right pinky. It really was his finger because it didn't have its nail. Leonardo had lost it in an accident at the farm. When he was distracted, a coffee pulping machine had almost torn off his finger when he was trying to fix it. A note written with newspaper letters said, "For being a tightwad. Next time we'll send the left one."

The criminals stopped calling for a few weeks. I spent the nights awake, and in those eight months I suffered much more than Leo because I felt that at any moment I would receive fatal news.

In my nightmares, I saw my body lying on Payares Peinado's desk and on my belly lay a small, black man. The general was lying back on a chair, smoking tobacco and tossing his pen into the air while the small man pressed into my stomach. Other times I dreamt that I was standing in front of the Archbishop's Palace and that a rider on horseback, whose face I couldn't recognize, came near to me to tell me a secret. I couldn't understand his whispers but it sounded similar to the jargon that Mr. Bremer, my neighbor in Río Verde, spoke when he chatted with me. If he was very tired, he became confused and thought he was speaking in Spanish but in reality he articulated his thoughts in his mother tongue.

I was afraid to sleep because even siestas were torture. One afternoon, I sat on a sofa near the phone. The small room, which had been turned into a place to receive calls, became a red stable. I thought I was dreaming and that I would wake, but I couldn't because it was impossible to close the doors of the place. A tiger came near and wanted to devour me. I defended myself from the attacks and other terrified animals, that were nearby, escaped. Deep down I repeated to myself that it was just a dream and that it would soon end. Luckily, I woke up and found myself bathed in blood. After turning fifty, my nosebleeds had become worse. In my purse I carried white hankies, but they didn't help much. Doctor Perdomo told me to keep out of the sun and rest.

La Repolla came to the house every day. Leo's wife had yelled "whore" at her in General Payares Peinado's office but she kept her mouth shut and ignored the insults. I continued to support Leo's two illegitimate kids and their mother. The general had suggested that I should try to calm down my legitimate daughter-in-law. He even said that maybe she was involved. Her jealousy knew no bounds, but I was sure that she wasn't capable of harming her husband as revenge. Rocío kept her place, and sometimes I thought her timidity was an act, but she was crazy in love with Leo and wouldn't betray him. Payares mistrusted *La Repolla* and he interrogated her a few times with the lie detector. She herself told me and swore she had nothing to do with the kidnapping.

The villains got in touch with me again and let me speak briefly with Leo. I felt he hated me because I didn't give them what they wanted and blamed me for his misfortune. They told me they would reduce the amount by twenty million but not to try anything before delivering the money. Even so, Payares Peinado told me to follow their instructions to the letter and that the secret service would do the rest. A cab took me to a neighborhood. I don't want to mention its name. In a blue leather briefcase I had the money wrapped in pages of *Cromos* magazine. I put it in a garbage can and left it there. I got back into the car and didn't look back. The driver, who was a plainclothes detective, accelerated, and we sped down the mountain so fast that I was sure we were going to crash.

When I got home Payares Peinado was on the phone.

"Señora, come to pick up your son," ordered the general.

I didn't know if he was alive or dead. When I saw him in the general's office, I almost didn't recognize him. For an instant I thought they had mistaken him for another hostage, but I knew he was my Leonardo because he was missing his little finger. It looked like they had shrunk him: he was like a ten year-old child with a beard like a Wandering Jew. My boy didn't even have teeth. He had lost over twenty kilos and his eyes and skin had a yellowish tinge. No doubt, I had to give him a lot of cod liver oil. His body gave off a musty odor. When he saw me he raised his head with no enthusiasm, covered his eyes with his right hand to protect himself from the light, and told me he was well. Then he started to cry.

All this time they had kept Leonardo in underwear and chained to a bed and only gave him one meal a day. They had taken away his clothes, gun, and identification documents, just in case he escaped. A woman, whom they called *La Mona*, the blond girl, was in charge of his food. At first they didn't allow him bathe or much less shave, but later they brought him water to wash his face. There was a latrine dug out in the floor for him to use, but this was practically impossible since he was always chained to the ramshackle bed. The room had no windows, and was barely big enough for two people. Leonardo counted the days during the first two weeks. However, soon he lost count and grew accustomed to the absence of the sun's rays. Leo thought he was in a basement because he heard laughter and steps above his head. Sometimes he heard dogfights on the streets and the voice of a salesman that repeatedly yelled, "Custard and buns." Leonardo never forgot the aroma of fresh bread that filtered into the basement. There was a bakery next to the house where they found Leonardo and the kidnappers made their calls from the pay phone installed there.

In the third month of the kidnapping, the woman who fed him gave him a newspaper. In it, it said that they didn't know where the young man who had been nabbed was being held. *La Mona* forced him to read the whole paper, even the classified ads, to her out loud since she said she was illiterate.

"See how the rich live. See, such elegant parties and we are living like rats. Your mother has a lot of dough, but she is very tough and won't give it up," she would tell him.

One day the woman took Leo a hand-drawn Parcheesi board. In the center she had drawn a heart. The two played for hours with beans that served as chips. She carried the dice in her bodice and told Leo that she warmed them there to bring her luck.

"My companions don't know what we are doing. I hope they don't find out because, otherwise, they'll hang us," she assured him.

La Mona didn't like this kind of life, but had to do it to please her boss. According to Leo, the girl was blonde and very beautiful. He hadn't seen her before and, because of her accent, thought she was from the coast. She told him of her childhood in a fishing village, and said that his face reminded her of her brother, who had drowned in the middle of some mangroves.

It took Leo time to get accustomed again to the light and the voices of other people. The general had explained that the kidnappers had set up *La Mona* as bait so that Leonardo wouldn't go crazy since he spent days without seeing or talking to anyone. Besides, she drew out information from him and even told him of a plan for his escape. When soldiers liberated Leonardo, he was sure she was his friend. His tears were not due to his feelings when he saw me, but because he found out that she had died during the shootout between the kidnappers and soldiers. For Leo, *La Mona* represented his only connection to the outside world. He had turned her into his goddess.

Not long after, I found out that the woman from the coast was my accountant's lover, who had planned the kidnapping. He was the leader of the band, and one of my servants kept him informed about all she heard in the house. One of the farm workers, who knew our daily routine, was one of the other accomplices.

Chapter XXIII

THE DECO FURNITURE

My fortune had been depleted by three fourths, but I still had the Los Álamos hacienda, five rental houses and my own car. After Fabio's death, I sold La Primavera and got rid of the cattle. The mansion on Bolívar Avenue required too much money, fors the servants' salaries, the gardener, and the driver, for its upkeep. So I divested myself of the servants, paid them for their years of service, and went to live in a smaller house. At my age, I didn't need luxuries, but I did need my rest. I kept the indispensable possessions and the rest of the furnishings, including the crystal lamps, were stored in Los Álamos. All these things had no importance. I clung to life, and if I wanted to live my last years to the fullest, then it was best to enjoy the simple things.

The termites devoured the last Deco style furniture. The green fabric of the cushions had rotten in the humidity, and the only thing that was left were the copper springs that could be seen through the holes in the armchairs. Dionisio's suitcases still had his name inscribed on them, as well as the stickers of airports and hotels. Small mice had gnawed the trunks lined in purple satin, and Dionisio's silk ties and bowties had been feasted on by thousands of cockroaches. The gloves and hats were passé but not for the spiders, who used the pearl embroidery to hide their eggs.

There were wood boxes filled with thousands of 78 rpm records, but they were useless because the leaks from the roof had soaked through the musical notes. Among the records there were some with women who smiled at the camera. One of them still had the inky traces of an autograph: "So that you don't forget me. Kika." In a corner was Eva Perón's photo and part of her face had faded into the chiaroscuro of the paper. The drawing of Beethoven, which Dionisio had brought from Chile, had still not been touched by rodent urine. The grand piano was quiet for several years, until a Presbyterian minister saw it at the farm and offered to buy it for his wife, who played and sang during their religious Sunday services. At the bottom of one of the commodes, there were packages of photos wrapped in plastic bags. Buried there were the faces of Jesús, Jesús María, Miguel, Israelino, Bárbara, Carmen, and my dear Rosario and her beloved Mister Stilman. My twins and Fabio, my little children, rested silently in the middle of some rotting sheets of paper. However, the only thing that was intact was my emerald green dress. It was still preserved in paper that had turned yellow. The mothballs were truly a blessing, because not even the insects had been able to finish off the dress.

On the white putty walls of the house of Los Álamos hung the diplomas of my kids, their medals, the bigger photographs of the family, Pope Pius XII and Pope John XXIII, a painting of the Bishop at a three quarter pose, the Divine Savior, the framed telegrams of the Ministry of Agriculture which confirmed the payment for Bellavista, and even a letter from Queen Fabiola of Belgium.

I had gotten in touch with King Baldvino's wife because she needed a formula for having a family. I sent the recipe for corn hair in white wine. In *Cronos* magazine I had read an article in which they talked about the queen's sadness because she couldn't produce heirs for her kingdom. Her Majesty thanked me with a postcard of the Brussels Royal Palace and we established a correspondence that lasted for many years. Her private secretary, someone called

Monsieur D'Cardan, wrote the typewritten letters and she signed each one. I imagined the queen in her office dictating to the *monsieur*, but I think her assistant was more excited than she was about being in contact with people he hadn't met and would never see. No doubt, for her it was part of her routine work, but I confess that I was always excited when I received Monsieur D'Cardan's messages.

A collection of over a hundred *Cromos* magazines, belonging to Marta María, was inherited by administrators of the farm. I had thrown them into the trash because they were in shreds. Even so, photos of Miss Universe, Luz María Zuluaga, or Rita Hayworth and any other celebrity were cut out and pasted on the walls. Once I saw the photo of Doña Bertha de Ospina, the former President of Colombia's wife disembarking from a plane, used to cover a hole in the kitchen wall. Many of the books that I accumulated during the years ended up being labyrinths for the ants that built their fortresses in the library and others were used as toilet paper by the farm hands.

Chapter XXIV

DAMARIS

My children's wild behavior had seriously depleted my family's assets and, even though my mind worked better than ever, my body didn't have the energy it needed to begin anew. Starting with that first surgery, when Doctor Perdomo removed three pounds of fat from my stomach plus a tumor as big as my fist, I realized that, little by little, my guts were starring to disintegrate. Doctor Perdomo predicted that I had two more years of life, but he was wrong because the agony was longer than I expected. Perhaps it was morbid on my part, but Doctor Perdomo was in a worse situation than I. In less than twenty four months, he was dead of liver cancer, though I believe it was due to cirrhosis because each time he came to the house to see me, his breath stank of *Cristal de Caldas* liquor.

In just a few years, the tumors began to grow in my abdomen and back; they grew at a terrible speed and were more powerful than my instinct for survival. I couldn't even smell cracklings or, much less, drink hot chocolate with a cornmeal cake; I vomited almost everything I ate but the worst part was trying to control the pain. I felt that the battle was against a ghost, and I wasn't used to fighting against a faceless enemy. My battles had been fought face-to-face, but I didn't know this damned battalion of termites that were destroying the house from the inside. I looked as weak as that jaguar cub that I once accidentally shot when I was out hunting with Jesús.

What I felt in my heart and stomach was the combination of a profound pain of my soul and body. I didn't know which of the two was worse: my sadness or the wild wish to once and for all end everything since I couldn't stand the physical pain. I think I had put up with too much without a complaint to the world or crying on a stranger's shoulder. I thought that my cancer was just the sum total of all the pain that I had accumulated in my lifetime. I felt like an enormous river rock that had always been in the same place but in which the water had made so many tunnels that it was only a shell of granite. In truth, I had suffered, but I didn't see myself as a victim of fatality since I had reinvented myself. If I had seen myself in the mirror, I had would have done so with dignity and a bit of vanity. I was proud of what I had built with Jesús and on my own. However, even though I knew I had been the founder of a lineage, I also knew that, with my death, my family was dying out.

I had planted and cultivated coffee, banana, guamo, orange, lemon and guanabana trees; cocoa, loofah, and chili plants, which I loved. I had also seen the Arabica and Bourbon coffee plants grow in my soil and, for years, they had produced millions of red seeds. I had had hundreds of barnyard fowl like chickens, roosters, guinea hens, turkies, geese, ducks, and peacocks. I don't know if my obsession with eggs had to do with the fact that, as a child, I only ate them during Lent and when my friend Nera gave them to me. In my farms the dogs had litters of ten puppies and the sows never stopped delivering piglets. The udders of my cows were always full of milk and the calves never stopped nursing. Tamales, plantains soup, beans, roast pork and cornmeal cakes, meat pie, and fritter made of flour, cheese and eggs were never missing from my table. Nobody left my home with an empty stomach. I told the maid to always prepare more food than what was needed, because anyone that visited me couldn't leave without a meal. The people who worked with me had to honor a rule that said it was far better for there to be too much than too little. Of course I had suffered from hunger in my childhood, and knew what it meant to visit the home of someone with means and go away with an empty belly.

Luckily, I had raised a family and had done my best to have an ideal home. I had paid my taxes, and had never taken a penny from anyone. I had created riches, but all I had done with my hands had been lost. Most probably this disease was the way of putting an end to my agony. But if Death came to visit me, we would encounter each other face to face. We would both die together and if there was resurrection then, we would rise together from the tomb to see Jesús and my other loved ones.

Finally, the doctor prescribed injections of morphine. In fact, the drug was only a palliative since the cancer didn't stop eating my guts and, as if that were not enough, tortured me every second. Damaris, the nurse, was with me day and night. The girl brought a small suitcase and stowed her personal items in a wardrobe that my daughter assigned to her. She was from Circasia, but lived with her mother in a room in the Las Setenta Casas neighborhood. Her mother took care of her one year old daughter. Her sister Amanda also shared the same room. Amanda was a teacher in a school in Córdoba and only saw her family on weekends. For three months she hadn't received her salary because the teachers were on strike, but she continued to teach because she was afraid of losing her job. Damaris's baby was the daughter of a radiologist of the Area Hospital, where she worked, but he was married and the father of twins. Even though he didn't acknowledge the little girl as his, he gave her a monthly stipend in order to avoid a lawsuit or public scandal.

Damaris had a charming figure and I don't doubt that even the hospital director could have fallen in love with her. Her eyes were blue and each time her hands touched my muscles I felt a lot of relief. Leonardo didn't take his eyes off her, and she didn't stop watching him either. Leo started visiting my house more frequently, but it wasn't only to ask about my health, but also to see Damaris. I was happy that, even if I was so ill, there was still room for love. Besides, I had all the time in the world to listen to the novels that one of my grandsons read to me. I was full of pity for the sufferings of *Siervo sin tierra* of Caballero Calderón, I detested the grandmother of *Cándida Eréndira*, and girl's apathy outraged me.

In a certain way, the story didn't amaze me because in Barcelona I met a girl who lived with her grandmother, a woman called Doña Blanquita. The child looked like an American actress who danced and had long ringlets. I remember that her name was Shirley Temple and her face was printed on a box of cookies that my daughter Marta María had sent me when she was in the United States. Doña Blanquita had a store that, during the day, sold petroleum and coal and, at night, was a bar. Well, the grandmother entertained her clients with her own granddaughter, who was thirteen. In the back of the house she had a room where she locked the girl in and forced her to receive her clients, who first got drunk on Póker beer, which she herself sold them. Her neighbors told me because they saw and heard everything through the bamboo that divided the two properties. Years later, I heard that Doña Blanquita was found with a knife in her stomach and it was said that her own granddaughter was the one who stuck it there. On the other hand, I didn't understand how Colonel Buendía could feed corn to his rooster, while he and his wife were starving. What the hell was retirement money for?

Before graduating from the nursing school in Manizales, Damaris had been employed as a dentist's secretary. She worked during the day in the office and studied at night. Her handwriting was impeccable and when I couldn't continue writing because I didn't even have the strength in my hands, she wrote what I dictated and then read it back to me.

On the 31st of December, 1990, at 3:25 in the afternoon, I decided to close my eyes and speak no more. This is the reason for my letter: Monsignor, I want you to carefully read this package of notes that I am sending by certified mail. Open it in ten years, when not even the ashes of my body will remain, when I will not exist in the memories of those whom I loved and who loved me. You can correct the spelling and modify the chapter where you appear with the nuns, if you wish, because it doesn't correspond with your true personality. In fact, if you feel that the readers would like to have an image of a Monsignor six feet tall and who, instead of admiring Napoleon, adores Alexander the Great, you can change it. It will not alter the significance of the events. But if you think that Sor Juana Inés de la Cruz gives it more prestige than San Juan de la Cruz you can include both, so that we can all be happy.

Now, please do not cut out the paragraphs that describe my son in law just because of the marijuana. Although it is not elegant to address these themes and others if they have to do with the family, I don't exaggerate nor write about my son in law in this manner because I hate him. If you need to confirm the facts, ask those who knew him in Armenia or his classmates from the Rufino High School. They will tell you about horrifying moments like, for instance, how this alcoholic and drug addict tormented my daughter.

I remember how my son in law had gotten a job working as a traveling salesman for *Mora Brothers*, a company that sold Singer sewing machines in installments. Marta María was about to give birth to her third child and he, so recklessly, went off to Apartadó, Chigorodó and other towns in Chocó. He disappeared for three months, and I had to take care of the delivery. When he returned to my daughter's house, she received him as if nothing had happened. I could never understand what attracted her to that man. No doubt he was handsome and women didn't leave him alone. But he wasn't a hard worker or very intelligent. He yelled at her, didn't stop humiliating her and, above all, beat her. In my house, she never saw such an example of mistreatment but she got used to his blows. I even thought that my son in law had a screw loose due to one of the many drunken sprees of his adolescence. But I was even more worried about the fact that my daughter was even crazier than he was since she continued to love him. The man even went so far as to send one of his best friends to see her while he was away on one of his famous sales trips. She herself told me and found out because the so-called friend of her husband later confessed it to her. The poor thing was so naive!

It turned out that that young man often visited her and brought her pastries. He comforted her and also played with the children. He took my grandchildren to the park and bought them ice cream. As time went by, he started to become seriously interested in her and suggested she leave her husband, that he would take charge of them all. Of course, he admitted that between the two of them, they had planned that he would seduce Marta María so that my son in law could get rid of her, because he was already living with another woman. The idea had been my son in law's, but his pal fell in love with my daughter. If he had one or more women, why didn't he separate from her? Only a dangerous lunatic could have invented and manipulated such a plan. But she only saw through the eyes of that man, one who wouldn't even give her the time of day. He only saw her legs when he wanted to go to bed with her or observed her face in detail when he turned it into a punching bag that received his fists.

After she finally left the beast and came with the children to live with me, she sat, with her legs tucked up to avoid the cold of the early hours of the morning, in a chair next to my bed. It was a rite that began at 5:30 in the morning: she got up, brought black coffee for both of us, and began talking nonstop about the dreams she had had the night before. She described to me all the places, people, and voices that she had seen and heard in her dream.

I interpreted them and told her all had signs of good omens. If she dreamed that she was trying on a diamond ring I responded that she was going to receive unexpected money. If she saw her brother Fabio, I asked her to pray because he was still suffering. If she herself was having a conversation with the nuns of La Presentación and didn't have on her uniform, I reminded her to write to them or call her friends from school. It was like a game because Marta María also interpreted my dreams. I remember it was one of the few intimate moments we had together. She spoke with me as if nobody else had ever listened to her. We gossiped, and she didn't stop talking about her ex-husband. He had done her so much damage and she didn't tell me before because she had been afraid of my reaction. In truth, it was as if she hadn't been born to be loved by a man. Love was not for all. Jesús would say "Love and shrouds fall from heaven". She was so in need of affection!

As for the kidnapping, I changed the real names of the people involved, except my son's. I did it because I want to keep a promise I made to General Payares, may he rest in peace. Some of those involved in the kidnapping died on the day I left the briefcase in the garbage can, and others are still walking on the streets of Armenia. One of the detectives was shot in the left leg and still limps. Over several months, I visited him in the hospital and he described the basement where my son was held. The neighbors never found out that a person was imprisoned there. Some told me that a woman with a child and husband had been living there for a year. At night there was a lot of activity in the house but the Blonde said her husband worked at the La María slaughterhouse and he had the early morning shift. The other details of this nightmare are contained in the summary.

If I had to live my life again I wouldn't change a thing, except some bitter moments: I wouldn't allow anyone to hit me as Domingo did, that despicable man with whom I left my aunt's house when I was an adolescent. I also wouldn't allow anyone to abuse or humiliate the poor. I wouldn't have had children that were born to die in my belly or of heart disease or sacrificed by the bullets of fate. I would marry Jesús again, have the same children, and five more. If my mother and father were alive, I would bring them to live with me, and I would give my children grandparents. I wouldn't tolerate my husband's infidelities. I would castrate him like a bull if I had to be miserable because of him. If I had to once again make my emerald green dress to use for only one hour of my life to celebrate my stepdaughter Rosario's wedding, I'd do it without thinking twice. I would put it away forever in mothballs. And, if I had to write my memoirs again, I would do it in the same way, because I want to leave a written statement of the life of a woman of the twentieth century that will serve as a testimony and lesson to others in similar circumstances.

Perhaps it won't be pointless, my dear Monsignor, that you should elaborate more on my moments of happiness. I was happy when I saw my aunt's cow grazing the grass in Don José María Giraldo's pastureland, I was overjoyed when I sucked on an egg and Nera told me stories about her mother. I remember Jesús's feline glances in Doña Nicasia's inn, the scarves that he brought me from Medellín and the avocados he used to mark his clothes. Jesús and I spent our honeymoon surrounded by ferocious beasts and he protected me in his arms like a hunter. He made me feel loved and hated. Deep down inside, I never could accept Jesús's philandering. He only gave me nonsensical excuses to see if I tolerated what to other women was like drinking a glass of sour milk and not getting indigestion. I don't know where Rosario got the fertility recipe and much less how the white wine used to prepare the drink reached my hands. I think the priest in Barcelona gave me some of his unconsecrated wine. Even though I remained without a drop of blood after my first son was born, I felt I was the happiest woman in the mountains when I held Dionisio in my arms. I was happy when Jesús rocked Dionisio and gave him a little kiss to calm his fever.

Black coffee in the morning, plantain soup with chili and cilantro at midday, beans with pork in the afternoons, milk with corn and brown sugar or crumbs of cornmeal cakes in a glass of milk were some of my favorite foods. I fed and gave water to the Indians of the mountains, to the blacks of the valley and the coast, to the peasants that occupied my lands, and to orphans and abandoned women. At Christmas I took pork, custard and fritter cheese with flour and eggs to the prisoners in jail. I can't deny that I was vengeful, authoritarian, and almost inflexible with my own errors and defects in others. I hated, like any other human being, but I intensely loved my dear ones.

Priests, nuns, Protestant ministers, lawyers, doctors and my children bled me of my money. But, in exchange, I was compensated with Doctor Orozco, Mister Bremer, the German-Jewish topographer, and you, dear Monsignor, who lent me the first books that I, Clara, read in my life. The last time I saw Doctor Hernando Orozco was a long time before I knew about my illness. I visited him in Medellín. He had been living separated from his wife for quite some time. His children were married, and he lived with a dog and an older woman who was in charge of cleaning, shopping, and giving him his medicines. I gave him a set of white sheets with his initials embroidered on them. I don't know if he used them, because he died a few months after my visit. That afternoon, when I arrived and knocked on the door, he was standing waiting for me, his maid holding his arm. He was as clean as if he was about to step into the operating room. I had never noticed that he stuttered but, in old age, his tongue had become heavier than a coal iron. He recognized me, but asked me how Jesús was.

"He died many years ago," I said, in a loud voice so he could hear me. "He died of a heart attack."

"How is Oooo…?" he took so long saying the first letter of my son's name that I had to finish the word Octavio.

"He also died of a problem with his heart." A sigh lodged in my throat and didn't see him again after that painful encounter.

I always asked myself what a doctor of his caliber was doing in these mountains. Jesús had brought him to the house because he didn't trust the midwives of the area. Virtudes, his first wife, had had a very bad time at the hands of the women of the hacienda who had helped her have her first children. He told me that, when Rosario was born, Virtudes had also had several hemorrhages, and that she never really recuperated from them. Jesús attributed the origin of Virtudes' mental illness to the midwife's clumsiness. That's why he brought Doctor Orozco from Medellín and convinced him to stay in these new lands. Besides, the doctor had fallen in love with one of the most beautiful women of Calarcá and Jesús had been the best man at their wedding. Truth be told, I don't think Doctor Orozco would have come on his own to these places looking to make a fortune with his profession. He was an honest doctor, an example of rectitude and wisdom. Many years later, after he separated from his wife, he returned to Medellín.

So, Dionisio introduced me to the world of music and by his side I listened to *Madame Butterfly, My Old San Juan* and *Oropel*. Leonardo had inherited his father's work ethic, and his unpredictable temperament. But in him was the love of the earth, including its females. He didn't want to study but, instead, dedicated himself to working the land and, together with Fabio, helped me a bit in administering the properties. Octavio, the twin, was like the childhood I didn't have and Fabio the mind I fed when I read my novels.

I enjoyed the afternoons when I saw my grandchildren play with colorful balloons and puppies full of fleas. I didn't like it when the pups slept with them because they shed hair in every corner, but I was charmed when they ran with the sow I bought them and she ended up sleeping on the bed with them. *Chachita*, the pig, had long eyelashes and would fall asleep when my grandkids scratched her back. I had to take her to Los Álamos, the first property I bought, because she got so fat that she was destroying the parquet floors of the mansion on the avenue. Even so, I took my grandchildren to the farm to see her in her new sty next to her new love.

As to Dionisio, I don't want to hurt him if he is still alive. I know he would regret hearing my voice, and would accuse me of being the reason for his failure. Tell him that I loved him a lot because I never told him, that I suffered more than he can ever know, and that I was always very proud of him and his music. I also forgive him for his resentment, his juvenile hatred against me, his shouts and threats, because I didn't give him what he always wanted. Tell him I was a mother like any other. I had defects as well as virtues. Please send him some money from the earnings of the publication of this memoir.